ONE WILD NIGHT

A HOLLYWOOD CHRONICLES NOVEL

A.L. JACKSON & REBECCA SHEA

A.L. Jackson
www.aljacksonauthor.com
Rebecca Shea
www.rebeccasheaauthor.com
Cover Design by RBA Designs
Editing by Kara Hildebrand at KLH Consulting
Formatting by Mesquite Business Services

Print ISBN: 978-1-946420-11-4
eBook ISBN: 978-1-946420-12-1

ONE WILD NIGHT

one
Kaylee

"Please tell me you're joking."

"Um…because this is a laughing matter?"

I almost laughed. Not because I was amused. Oh no. I was not. More like horrified.

Because here I was, sitting in a limo. Alone. Staring out the window at the red carpet that loomed ahead. A red carpet littered with celebrities who milled around like it was commonplace and not some kind of alternate universe.

Somebody kill me now.

I pressed my cell a little harder to my ear, head beginning to shake as my stomach flopped with nerves. "Are you crazy? There is no way I'm going in there by myself."

"Oh, come on, Kaylee. It's not any different than going to the movies on a Friday night."

Elle's voice took on that casual tone she used whenever she wanted to get her way, the words missing the frantic edge they'd held when she'd first called me to tell me she wasn't coming.

To her father's directorial premiere.

Okay. So, it wasn't his first movie. Eleanor Ward had grown up in Hollywood, her father directing and producing some low-budget, albeit freaking fantastic movies. There was hardly any shame in that.

But this…this was the big one, an A-list cast and a budget to match.

So yeah. It was a Friday night.

And I was at the movies.

But come on. Who was she kidding? We both knew there was absolutely no comparison.

"Don't do that," I hissed.

"Don't do what?" she returned, all kinds of innocent.

"That *thing* you do. Where you act like nothing is a big deal when you know as well as I do it's a *really* big deal."

Exasperation blew through the words.

Ugh.

Elle.

She just had this way about her, always going about life as if nothing in the world mattered. Everything a game. No consequences or feelings or fears involved.

Easy.

It was as if she held the entire world in the palm of her hand. Every room she walked into, she owned. Every conversation, she commanded.

All of it with a flick of her hand and a twitch of her smile.

Magnetic.

I'd recognized her type the second she waltzed into the dorm we'd shared our freshman year at UCLA.

Gorgeous.

Spoiled.

Rich.

Sucking on a silver spoon when I'd worked my fingers to the bone for every scholarship I could possibly win. She had been subjected to *dorm* life because her daddy wanted her to experience *real* life, sent to slum it up with the common folk for an entire year.

Poor thing.

But I soon discovered beneath all that entitlement was a girl who would drop it all on a dime for those she cared about. Without a second thought.

So maybe we were polar opposites, but it didn't take long for us to become attached at the hip.

That was ten years ago.

In all that time, she'd never let me down.

Not until today.

"Please, Kaylee," she whispered, and that desperation was weaving its way back in. "I already hate that I'm doing this to Daddy. Both of us can't not show. He'll be devastated." Her voice dropped to a whisper. "And this is *important*."

What could be so important that she wasn't here?

I pressed the heel of my hand to my eye, probably messing up the thick liner and black mascara I'd spent way too much time fretting over. "I don't understand how you could do this to me or to him. Tell me what's going on."

"I'll explain it all later. I just..." There was rustling in the background, muffled voices, before her attention came back to me. "I have to go. Just...please do this for me. Please, Kay Kay?"

I could almost see her big, brown puppy dog eyes pleading from across the space.

Wherever the hell that was.

Surrender.

It was there in my sigh.

"Fine. But you owe me big."

She gushed in relief. "I know. I know. Anything, and it's yours. Tell Daddy I love him, and I'm really sorry. I'm sure he'll be over to kick my ass in the morning."

"You know he will."

The limo, the one Elle had sent for me, mind you, after she'd begged and pleaded and convinced me that I *had* to be here with her, inched forward. She'd been adamant that I couldn't miss this, that I was family, and it didn't matter that I didn't belong here at all.

And here I was.

Nervous energy prickled across every inch of my exposed skin as the attendant opened the door, that red carpet now right at my awkward feet.

I sucked in a breath and pasted on a fake smile, praying I could pull this off.

One night.

I could do this.

I could pretend as if I didn't wobble on my five-inch heels as I stepped out into the night. Pretend I felt confident in this over-the-top, super-sexy dress with the slit running all the way to the top of my thigh. One I'd borrowed from Elle because God knew I couldn't afford it on my kindergarten teacher salary. Pretend the flashes of cameras didn't blind my eyes.

I kept my head down as I moved forward.

"Julianne. Julianne Hough. Over here."

Um. What?

Wide-eyed, I looked back over my shoulder. Yeah. Not so much.

I bit back a cringe when the reporter, one whose face I'd seen plastered too many times on my TV because Elle was addicted to celebrity TV, mouthed, "Oh sorry," and turned away in favor of someone much more interesting.

God.

Could anything be more humiliating?

I had the urge to kick off my heels and run. Cower and hide and slink into my safe little world where I'd be curled up on my couch with a glass of wine and a good book.

I glanced to the right.

A hundred feet ahead, the darkened double doors of the theater teased me with the promise of its sanctuary. All I had to do was make it inside unnoticed. I'd slip in, be present for Elle's father, Roger Ward, who was one of the nicest guys I knew, and then as soon as the credits rolled, I'd get the hell out of Dodge.

I tucked my chin to my chest, eyes trained on my feet, my uncoordinated, clumsy, strides just short of a run.

Just get inside. Just get inside.

A gasp of shocked air shot from me when I slammed into a wall.

A very, very hard wall.

A wall made up of flesh and muscle, and my feet were sliding out from under me as I went reeling back. Strong hands darted out, cinched around my upper arms to keep me from falling, drawing me up close.

So, so close.

I had the sudden, overwhelming urge to bury my nose deeper into that big wall of chest because it just smelled so damned good.

Or maybe I only wanted to bury my face in it, so I'd fall in and completely disappear. Because this had to rank up there as one of the most mortifying moments of my entire life, second only to the time my shorts caught on the slide in fourth grade and they split right up the middle.

Warily, I peeked up at my savior.

Breath gone.

Eyes wide.

Stomach a mixed-up pool of desire and embarrassment on the floor.

An earth-shattering smile full of bright white teeth had my heart rate shifting into high gear, but it was the playful brown eyes full of mischief and sex that had my knees knocking.

Oh, God.

Yes, yes, I had my answer. Things could be so much more humiliating.

Because I'd just run headfirst into Paxton Myles.

two

Paxton

The look of sheer terror on her beautiful face makes it hard to contain my chuckle. My fingers wrap around her thin arms as she struggles to find her feet and tries to balance on her ridiculously too-high heels. I can feel her body tremble under my fingertips, and her lips form a perfect *O* as recognition flashes across her face.

I smile down on her, and she slams her mouth shut just as her cheeks fill with color. I usually have that effect on women. Glad to see she's not any different.

It was impossible not to notice her the moment she stepped out of that limo. Her long blonde hair, her petite frame, and the anxious way she ran from the paparazzi and fell right into my arms.

My thumbs rub the soft skin of her arms, and the scent of her floral perfume is intoxicating.

"Hey, hey, easy now," I joke with her as she presses her hands against my chest and regains her composure. Her eyes flutter closed, and she takes a deep breath, but I can't help but notice her hands shaking and her full lips twitching nervously.

Realizing what's just happened, she exhales softly. "God, I'm so sorry," she mumbles under her breath, shuffling from foot to foot as she tries to straighten her long, black dress that has shifted during her stumble.

"The cameras can be intimidating." I try to calm her and ease her obvious anxiety. "But I'm pretty sure that stumble is going to make the highlight reel on tonight's tabloid television."

I laugh openly and her cheeks turn a darker shade of red. "I'm Pax." I grin, holding out one hand for her to shake while my other still holds her upright. "And you are?"

Her eyes fall to my outstretched hand only she doesn't reciprocate. "I know who you are," her voice rattles. "I'm not a celebrity. I'm a kindergarten teacher."

She finally manages to shrug out of my grip, and I hold both hands up in a show of surrender. She lifts her chin and finally holds eye contact with me in mock confidence. I can see how fucking nervous she is by the little dance she's doing and it's making my dick hard. I love it when I can make women squirm.

The flush from her cheeks is now crawling down her neck and onto her chest. It's hard not to follow those red splotches down to her perfectly lifted tits—tits that would fit nicely in the palm of my hands.

"Name. What's your name?" I lift my head from her breasts up to her face as I wait for her to answer. She fumbles around awkwardly, juggling her small clutch from hand to hand.

"Kaylee. Kaylee Rose."

I see Kendall Scott, my publicist, over Kaylee's shoulder, one of her perfectly sculpted eyebrows arched in curiosity, but a look of warning shoots from her bright blue eyes. A look she's always giving me.

I give her a little wink and decide to ignore her non-verbal warning, turning my attention back to Kaylee.

"Nice to meet you, Kaylee Rose."

She inhales sharply at the sound of her name rolling off my tongue. I've yet to lose the Southern accent I acquired growing up in Texas. It's my secret weapon. Women find it hard to resist that accent, and it's helped me more often than it's hurt me.

My agent has spent thousands on dialect coaches, telling me it'll make me more marketable when I'm able to ditch that light Southern drawl, but I know when to use it, and when I need to turn up the charm. I hold my hand out again for her to take and she hesitates for just a moment before sliding her soft hand in mine.

Kaylee is adorable and horribly uncomfortable, and I can't help but find it perfectly amusing. She nods her head frantically as her eyes dart around me and toward the large theater doors she was so adamant to get to when she fell face first into me.

Pulling her hand from mine, she fakes a smile. "Nice to meet you too," she mutters as she scurries away, glancing back over her delicate shoulder at me.

"Enjoy the movie, Kaylee." I laugh openly as she hurries inside.

"What the hell was that?" Philip Montes asks as he sidles up next to me, sipping a glass of champagne. He's breaking public relations cardinal rule number one; don't be photographed with alcohol. He catches me looking at the crystal glass in his hand and shrugs before taking a sip of bubbly.

"I'm not entirely sure, but I'm about to find out." I see the large double doors close behind her.

"She's not Hollywood," he scoffs and steps aside as Jenna Berg and Ashton Walters make their way toward us down the red carpet.

"No. No, she's not. Which makes me all the more interested," I reply, also stepping aside. Jenna and Ashton are the new "it" couple in Hollywood. Cameras flash, blinding me. I take this as my cue to get the hell inside and away from this red carpet.

"I give them five months," Philip says under his breath, his eyebrow rising as we watch the power couple work the red carpet. "I'm ninety-nine percent sure he plays for both teams."

I openly laugh, because I'm ninety-nine percent sure Philip is right.

Philip has been my best friend and confidant in this wild business. We've co-starred in three movies together, and both of our careers took off simultaneously. We've been dubbed the modern-day Matt Damon and Ben Affleck—a whole lot to live up to, but we're definitely up to the challenge.

Philip and I follow the growing crowd toward the dark theater. After we check our phones in, protocol for all screenings and premieres, we find our way toward the assigned seats that await us in the front row.

It's hard not to notice Kaylee, sitting in the roped off area just across the row from me, where typically only actors, directors, and producers are allowed. She sits with her legs carefully crossed and her hands resting on her knee—so proper.

It's when I see Roger Ward, our director, approach her with a smile before leaning down and pulling her into an embrace that my curiosity is even more piqued.

She knows Ward.

Interesting.

Ward's wife, Lindsay, also greets Kaylee warmly. All three share in conversation, laughing before Roger Ward points to the seat next to Kaylee. A moment passes between them before the smile suddenly falls from Mr. Ward's face. It's a look of disappointment. I've seen it many times, only this time it's not directed at me.

Kaylee cringes, as she pulls her bottom lip between her teeth. Both Mr. and Mrs. Ward look upset, but not at Kaylee. A few more words are exchanged and another brief embrace before they sit down in the row directly in front of her. They both occasionally turn around to make small talk before the lights begin to flicker, and it's easy to see Kaylee begin to visibly calm.

Philip and I take our seats as the lights begin to dim and then rise again in an effort to get everyone to quiet down, but I can't help but notice the empty seat next to Kaylee.

A round of applause fills the theater as Roger Ward stands and makes his way to the front to address the audience.

I try to sit still as the movie starts, as the scenes play. It's impossible. I decide to make my move. I nod my head toward Kaylee and Philip rolls his eyes, but not before he fist bumps me.

It takes me three steps to get to her. Three steps before her bright blue eyes look up at me. Three steps is all it takes for me to decide that this girl is going to be mine.

three

Kaylee

That accent.

God.

That accent.

It was nothing less than a weapon, and I couldn't help but feel as if I'd been slayed. A steel blade straight through the heart. Or maybe I'd been struck by an arrow from one of the super cute cupid bows. With the way things were going down right now? Anything was possible.

I stumbled the rest of the way into the theater. I made sure to keep one eye open, footsteps cautioned, because I sure as hell didn't need a repeat of five seconds ago. As it was, my insides were already twisted into a million unrecognizable knots, and I was pretty sure there was only one thing that could get them *undone*.

This mess of embarrassed nerves? They had amplified into a bundle of this throbbing, unrelenting attraction that shivered across my skin.

Of course, I'd known the chances of seeing him tonight tipped the scale to high. I mean, come on. He was the freaking star of the movie.

But I thought it'd be with Elle at my side. Me, the invisible sidekick, the ordinary, plain girl hiding behind her friend's bold presence like it was a shield.

Unnoticed.

But no. Because it was me, I had to go and trip into the arms of the one man who held the power to make me tremble through the screen.

Everyone had a Hollywood crush. A free card. A fantasy.

Yes.

Paxton Myles was mine.

But those fantasies were never supposed to manifest themselves as seductive flesh and strong hands and megawatt smiles.

They weren't supposed to flirt.

I mean, that's what he was doing, wasn't it? Or had my subconscious—screaming at me to go ahead and just take the plunge and drop the rest of the way to his feet—convinced me into believing he might have an interest in me?

Stop it, I berated myself, because those were lines of thought I definitely didn't need to entertain. Even if he was interested, I absolutely was not. Flings were not my style, and they were never going to be.

Within the shelter of the theater, I shoved it all down, took a steeling breath as I checked in, and made my way to the seat I'd been assigned. I did my best to keep the slit of my dress from exposing too much leg as I settled into my seat up close to the screen.

Yeah.

That was impossible.

Roger Ward met my eye from the group of people he and his wife, Lindsay, were chatting with. He wandered my way, eyes scanning as he approached.

"Kaylee, it's so nice to see you. Thank you for coming. You don't know what it means to me."

He held me by both hands, and I leaned forward to receive the kiss he placed on my cheek.

"I wouldn't have missed it."

His smile was sincere, and he squeezed my hands tighter,

glancing around again. "Where's that daughter of mine?"

I cringed.

He caught it, and his smile tipped down, lines pulling across his strong brow. "What happened?"

I shook my head, trying to assuage the worry that was so clear. "She's totally fine," I said way too fast, before I slowed to clarify. "But apparently some sort of emergency came up."

The last came out like a question, because how did you explain away the antics of Eleanor Ward?

Clueless, my shoulders lifted. "She called me just as my limo was pulling up. She promised she would explain everything to us tomorrow, but she told me to tell you how sorry she is that she's not here."

Questions flashed across his features, and I squeezed his hands a little tighter. "I promise. She wasn't hurt or anything like that. Please…just enjoy your night. She already feels awful, and I know she doesn't want you worrying about her."

Frustration held fast for a fleeting second, before he seemed to swallow it down. "Well, I guess we can't do anything about it now. And you know Elle. She's doing whatever it is she really thinks she needs to be doing."

I smiled with a light chuckle. "Exactly."

Lindsay came up behind him, gave me a quick hug, and the two of them settled into their seats directly in the row in front of me.

Again, I was struck with just how crazy it was that I was here. I could be annoyed. Irritated with Elle for talking me into coming then turning around and bailing.

But no.

I pushed all that aside and instead sent a silent thank you to my best friend. I never would have the opportunity to experience something like this without her.

I chatted with Roger and Lindsay for a couple minutes before he went up front to introduce the movie.

When he returned to his seat, the lights dimmed.

A shiver of excitement rolled through me. I tried to pretend it wasn't at the thought of seeing Paxton Myles on the big screen and knowing he was in the room.

Nope.

Didn't matter at all.

Music thundered through the surround sound, vibrating the ground, the intro a no holds barred attention grabber.

Enraptured by the English scenery, I leaned forward, my hand over my chest.

Roger Ward was truly brilliant.

And by God, so was the face that entered the screen. It was an outright crime for a man to look as good as Paxton Myles, and now I knew first hand it wasn't just photoshopping and lighting.

So maybe in this film he was playing eighteenth century English Royalty.

None of that really mattered.

Because the man was a freaking Greek God.

The air stirred, a whoosh of quieted activity at the empty seat that was supposed to belong to Elle.

My breath hitched. I struggled not to inhale, struggled not to look. Struggled to pretend as if I wasn't hit with an overwhelming urge to turn and bury my nose in that masculine scent I could feel prodding at my senses.

The way my chest was heaving and my hands curled around the armrests had to have been obvious enough.

Suddenly he was there, pushing into my personal space, his mouth at my ear. His Southern accent that had me in a puddle earlier was now twisted to match the character on the screen. "He's a good-looking bloke, isn't he?"

I had to shake my head to clear it of the stupor. My chin tipped up toward him, my eyes narrowed in a scowl. "Excuse me?" It came out an accusation.

He just sent me one of those belly-flipping grins, the magnitude of it lit up in the frames flicking across the screen. "That bloke there on the screen. You seemed a little...impressed."

"Um, wow. Someone's full of themselves, aren't they?"

I sent the words with all the confidence I could muster, hoping they would knock him down a notch.

His cockiness just grew. Those full lips tweaked into a smirk. "Oh, Kaylee Rose. Don't act like I couldn't tell you wanted to climb right over these chairs and fall into that screen. And here I am, in the flesh. No need to go pretending when you can have the real deal."

"Shh." It was all a frantic whisper, my eyes wide and wild as they jumped to Roger and Lindsay, praying they weren't noticing who'd slithered up to my side.

God. Did the man have no shame?

His hand found the slit on my dress, his fingertips light, so, so light I had to wonder if he was really even touching me. Still, the energy eliciting a cascade of chills, an illicit feeling washing me in thigh-clenching desire.

"I like your dress." He whispered it like a tease.

Nope.

No shame whatsoever.

He inched closer, and I lost all my breath. My hands clutched tighter to the armrests, and I gave it my all to keep my breaths from panting out of my lungs.

"Stop it," I hissed.

"Stop what?" Oh yes, he could play it off as all kinds of innocent. But I could see the mischief glinting in the brown of his eyes.

"Stop trying to get a rise out of me."

"Is that what I'm doing? Getting a rise out of you? I'm fairly certain it's the reverse."

Gah. I wanted to scream. The man was incorrigible.

Roger Ward slanted us a curious glance.

My voice was hardly a breath. "You're making a scene."

His fingers fluttered up, not quite touching me. Not until they were right over the thunder stampeding beneath my ribs. He caressed at the v of my low neckline, right between my breasts. "I like making scenes. Obviously. And right now, I want to make one with you."

"Not a chance."

"Oh, I beg to differ. I'd put down good money that there are all kinds of *chances* rolling around in that pretty little head of yours."

"You don't know me."

"But I will."

I gulped around the lump in my throat, focused ahead, on the screen. Of course, the infuriating man just teased me from there. Time spun on like the best kind of torture, my breaths shallow and my lungs heavy, butterflies flitting this way and that as I watched the romance play out on the big screen.

Intense.

Deep.

Sexy.

His voice was back to whispering, lips brushing the shell of my ear. "Pay close attention, Kaylee Rose. We're getting to the good part."

My legs went weak as the film slanted into the shadows of a bedroom, the moon all aglow to illuminate one of the sexiest, hottest love scenes I'd ever seen, seductive and slow, and there was nothing I could do to keep from envisioning that mouth sliding down my neck and delving between my breasts.

I squirmed in my seat.

For that scene alone, Paxton Myles deserved an Academy Award.

Hell. Who was I kidding? I doubted there was any acting involved. It didn't take a lot of imagination to figure out Paxton Myles knew his way around the bedroom.

A gush of air left me as the scene closed.

A dark chuckle, so low, filtered around me like a hot breeze. "Someone seems...affected."

Mouth dry, I swallowed. "It was a beautiful movie."

I meant it, in all honesty. I was incredibly proud of Roger. And as much as I didn't want to be, I was completely awed by Paxton.

Another rogue grin. If I wasn't already sitting, it would knock me from my feet. "Not quite as beautiful as you."

Soft, disbelieving laughter left me on a sigh. "You know, you don't need to patronize me."

For the first time, something serious flashed through his expression. "I'm not a liar, Kaylee Rose, nor do I have the time or inclination to patronize women. When I tell you you're beautiful, I mean it."

Redness seeped across my chest and climbed to my cheeks.

God. This man.

"Then I apologize." I stood, straightened my dress as Roger and Lindsay were standing. "If you'll excuse me," I said, turning all my attention on the Wards, my escape.

Paxton didn't stand. Of course, he didn't. Instead he made me nearly crawl across his lap to make my way out.

Roger met me at the end of the aisle. "What did you think?"

I swallowed down the flush I could feel still coloring my face. "I thought it was phenomenal. The best thing I've ever seen."

"Oh, you don't need to play it up on my account."

My thoughts flashed to the parting words I'd shared with Paxton.

"I'm not." I swore it like a solemn oath. "I felt it everywhere. It's unforgettable."

Pride simmered on the man's face, and Lindsay tucked her head on his shoulder, patted his chest. "I told you," she said. "It's perfection."

I felt the intensity of the stare boring into me, and I pushed a smile to my face and fiddled with a strand of hair. "Thank you so much for having me. I'm going to head out."

Roger tsked. "You can't leave yet. We'll be leaving for the after party in just a few minutes."

"Oh, I think I'm going to pass."

I needed to get out of there and now. Because all I wanted was to turn and look over my shoulder, to seek out the distinct laugh reverberating through the air, the mesmerizing sound coming from the man who'd completely captivated me.

My fantasy was a little too close to reality for my comfort zone.

My jammies and a big tub of ice cream were definitely calling to me. It was time to come back down to earth.

"Rubbish," Roger said, giving a good go at his best English accent. "You have to come. You've only gotten half the experience of a premiere. You need a taste of the entire thing."

Energy stirred, and I sucked in a breath, that presence engulfing me as Paxton edged up to bring his chest to my back, words a whisper in my ear. "Yes, you definitely need to get a taste of the entire thing. God knows I want a taste."

ONE **WILD** NIGHT

Oh, Lord.
I was in trouble.
So, so much trouble.

four

Paxton

The limo door slams closed behind me as I slide onto the leather seat with a loud sigh. My dick pitifully throbs in my pants as I think about Kaylee and her soft skin that I was able to chance a brief touch.

How the fuck does a girl I've never met, never seen before, stumble into my arms and have this effect on me?

I'm Paxton Myles. I can have any woman in Hollywood, or better yet, the free world. Yet, a fucking petite blonde kindergarten teacher who literally trips into my arms is what's causing my dick to react this way.

Shit.

I shake my head at myself.

I shift uncomfortably, adjusting myself, and reach for the bottle of whiskey from the wet bar. Tossing a few ice cubes into the crystal rocks glass, I serve up a healthy pour of the alcohol.

That dress.

Those legs.

Her perfect tits.

Fuck.

I close my eyes, pitching my head back against the leather seat as visions of her assault me. I grumble as thoughts of Kaylee dance around my head. Thoughts of her legs wrapped around me fill my mind, and my dick throbs harder. I envision the feel of her nipples pebbling in my mouth as my tongue laps circles around her sweet flesh.

Pressing the crystal glass to my mouth, I slam the smooth amber liquid and purse my lips as I swallow hard. I blow a puff of hot air from my lungs and grit my teeth before pouring another two fingers of premium whiskey into the empty glass. I shake my head as the warm, rich liquid settles into my stomach.

I remember my father telling me whiskey is meant to be sipped…enjoyed. Not slammed.

However, right now, I need something to take the edge and my mind off the beautiful Kaylee Rose. Something to kill the sinful thoughts I'm having of Kaylee right now; on top of me, underneath me…pressed against a wall. "Fuck," I mutter to myself and brush my hand over my face.

As the limo rolls to a stop, the sound of Whitney Brenna's soft moans fill the car. I chance a glance to my right and see Philip has his hand up her dress and his lips pressed to her neck. My man has been wanting to tap Whitney since he co-starred with her on some daytime soap opera over a year ago.

I scoot toward the door, doing the best to adjust my semi-hard dick before the paparazzi catch a picture of my boner. "Game time," I tell myself as I exit the limo, stepping out into the tepid Los Angeles air.

I straighten my bow tie and button my suit coat. With the tilt of my head, I flash the million-dollar smile that's made me rich, and I saunter into the Hollywood Highlands Hotel.

The after party is in full swing. Not an expense was spared— as usual. Gift bags line long tables for the guests to take, and I watch ladies elbow each other for the chance to get their hands on one. The swag bags are always a hit with the non-industry people.

The sound of laughter fills the large, open room. I smile politely and nod as people congratulate me on my performance in passing. A few stop to talk me up, and I do my best to appear interested, when in actuality, I don't give two fucks about their assessment of my acting.

With my fake smile plastered on, I stare blankly at them, casually looking over their shoulders and through the sea of bodies in hopes of seeing my girl. *My girl.* Even if she's mine for only one night. Presumptuous of me? Probably. But I don't give a shit. I have one goal in mind tonight and that's Kaylee Rose.

The open bar ensures that alcohol is flowing and people stand around in small groups talking and laughing. This is the best part of this business—the parties, the booze, the women.

Across the room, I finally catch a glimpse of Kaylee. Her back pressed firmly to a wall, a glass of wine clutched between both of her hands. Kaylee is deep in conversation with Lindsay Ward when I make my way over to them.

"Ladies," I say, announcing my approach. Wrapping an arm around Lindsay Ward's shoulders, I lean into her. "Looking as beautiful as ever tonight, Mrs. Ward." She shakes her head and laughs.

"You are such a charmer, Paxton." She pats my chest and leans into me. "Here, I'd like you to meet Kaylee Rose. This is Eleanor's best friend."

Lindsay tugs on Kaylee's arm, pulling her closer to us. So close I can smell her floral perfume. So close I can almost feel her soft skin. So close, but not close enough for what I need from her.

"And thank goodness she's responsible and actually showed up tonight. I don't know what has gotten into Elle lately," her voice trails off, not that I was really listening anyway. I've been lost in Kaylee since she fell into my arms. Everything else has been a mere distraction. "You two were quite chatty during the movie," she says, one of her eyebrows arching in curiosity. "Have you two met before?"

It's easy to see Kaylee's cheeks flush a bright shade of pink at our introduction. She refuses to look up at me and keeps her eyes cast down at the glass of wine that her long, lean fingers twirl in her hands.

"Oh yes, we've already met," I announce proudly, hoping Kaylee will finally look at me. She doesn't. *Shit.*

"You have, when?" Lindsay questions, taking a step back.

"Earlier this evening. It was hard to miss Kaylee's entrance."

Kaylee looks up from her glass of wine and narrows her eyes at me.

"I know darling, she's stunning, isn't she?" Mrs. Ward asks, patting Kaylee on the arm.

"She certainly is," I answer her and smile at Kaylee, who hasn't removed the scowl from her face.

"You're both being too kind," Kaylee says. "Lindsay, I know Elle is disappointed she couldn't be here. We both knew how much this evening meant to Roger. I'm sure she has a really good reason for not making it."

Mrs. Ward openly scoffs, but slams her champagne glass against her lips to stop herself from saying anything further.

"And Mr. Myles, it was a pleasure meeting you." Kaylee rolls her eyes at me and tosses back the last of her wine. "Congratulations on your movie. Stunning work as always."

You can literally hear the sarcasm roll of her tongue with each word. Mrs. Ward looks between us and purses her lips, confused by Kaylee's sudden shift in moods. "But if you two will excuse me, I have to be going. I have to be up early." She hands me her empty glass. "You don't mind handling that for me, do you?" She smirks.

"Of course." I hold out the empty glass, and it's immediately removed by a passing server. What a little vixen. She's trying to put me in my place.

"Oh, that's how it's done." She rolls her eyes at me, and I smirk. I love feisty Kaylee.

"What's going on with you two?" Mrs. Ward asks us with a smile. She steps back slowly and crosses her arms to get a better look at the both of us. Kaylee rubs her hands over her arms nervously and glares at me.

"Nothing!" Kaylee spits out before I have a chance to come up with something witty. Dammit. She's quick to the punch. I need to step up my game.

"Are you sure you two haven't met before tonight?"

"No!" Kaylee blurts out, and I can't help but laugh. I love seeing her squirm.

"No, Mrs. Ward. We haven't," I finally offer, hoping Kaylee will calm down. With a little shake of my head, I continue speaking to Lindsay, but turn my attention to Kaylee. "But while it was certainly an unexpected introduction, it was not unwelcome. In fact, I hope for the chance to get to know her better."

"Oh, she's fantastic," Lindsay pipes in. I don't bother to turn my attention back to her as she continues to sing Kaylee's praises. I remain focused on the beautiful woman in front of me. "She's smart, and kind, and such a great friend to Elle..." Lindsay continues.

I don't hear anything else she says. With her head tilted and the slightest hint of a smile turning up the corner of her mouth, Kaylee watches me. She's succumbed to the famous Paxton Myles smile and charm that I'm known for. She exhales softly and finally lets her lips twist into a small smile.

"The night is young. Let's go get a drink, shall we, Kaylee?"

five
Kaylee

What in the world was I allowing this man to do to me? Every time I tried to shut him down, he just shot me that smirk that had my stomach doing three-sixties.

Complete flip-flops, pulled in one direction only for my defenses to go careening the opposite. Shoving him off only to be right back where I started—staring up into the mesmerizing, playful eyes I couldn't help but want to get lost in.

"I guess I could stay for one more drink," I found myself saying, knowing it was such a stupid, bad idea, but unable to resist the charm that was this man.

What could one drink hurt?

"I'll talk to you later, Mrs. Ward," I said, and she gave me a look that both told me to have fun and warned me all the same.

Paxton threaded his fingers through mine.

Oh my God.

It was then I was certain one drink could cause all kinds of mayhem. That every second spent in the presence of this man was a hazard. I had completely underestimated his draw. Because with just that innocent touch, my heart raced and sped, just as fast as the tingles that spread up my arm.

Lord, help me.

Like a love-struck fool, I trailed him across the extravagant space. Every movement he made was filled with confidence and ease. The man owned the room. Heads turned in his wake. Clearly, everyone was just as compelled by him as me.

But it was the curious glances cast my way that had me ducking my head, tucking my chin to my chest.

The last thing I needed was to be the target for some misconstrued gossip.

I followed him to the long, darkened bar, the large bottles of expensive liquors illuminated by white neon lights that reflected against the mirrored glass of the back-bar that rose high above the bartender.

A bartender who, of course, wore a long sleeved white button down and black vest.

It was all so very Hollywood chic, and again I was wondering how in the world I'd found myself in this position.

His voice was low at my ear. "What would you like to drink?"

"A Riesling would be nice."

He turned to the bartender. "Riesling for the lovely lady. Whiskey for me."

The bartender poured our drinks, and Paxton passed mine to me. He lifted his tumbler with a subtle tilt my direction, our glasses clinking as he made a toast. "To this magical, unforgettable night."

His words were packed with innuendo, and I nearly choked as I took a sip of my wine. A blush I couldn't fight streaking everywhere, this unfound attraction spreading far and fast.

Stupid girl.

Casually, he set his hip against the bar. "So, tell me, Kaylee Rose, how is it you know Eleanor Ward and her family? You seem a little...out of place."

I felt my brow draw. "What's that supposed to mean?"

I wanted to be offended, but his observation wasn't any different than what I'd been thinking all night.

He chuckled, the sound so seductive all those secret places inside me clenched with desire.

Damn him.

He edged closer, and when he spoke, his breath washed over

me like a delicious breeze. "Oh, come on, beautiful girl, there's no need to play coy. You're much too sweet to belong in the midst of all these vultures. They'd rip you to shreds."

Arching a brow, I leaned back and met his eyes. "Vultures? You mean vultures like you?"

He laughed, deep and low, the man encroaching into my space, towering over me as he dipped his nose to run it along my hairline and down to my ear. "I'd gladly tear you apart, Kaylee Rose. But I promise you, it will be in the very best way. So good, in fact, you'll be begging me to do it again and again."

Shivers skated along my flesh.

Shit. Shit. Shit.

There was no question in my mind he'd make good on his promise.

A dangerous, dangerous fantasy.

That's what this was.

Too close for comfort.

I cleared my throat. "Elle and I were roommates during our first year at UCLA." Affection laced with irritation filled up my tone. "She's definitely from a different world than I am." I gave an offhanded, helpless shrug. "But somehow, we became best friends through it all."

He raked his teeth over his bottom lip. "Opposites do attract, and all of that."

Yep.

More innuendo.

And again, I felt shaky and itchy, wanting to lean forward to inhale the essence of his man, all the while wanting to run before I fell into his trap.

Right then, running sounded like the best plan.

I stepped back and downed my wine, set the glass on the bar. "If you'll excuse me."

I rushed for the hallway and into the ladies' restroom, pressed my hands to the counter, and stared at myself in the mirror as I tried to calm my rapid breaths.

Paxton Myles was so absolutely right.

I didn't belong here.

I was out of place. Ignorant. Just begging to be slaughtered. But it wouldn't be at the hands of anyone else at the after party.

It would be at the hands of a man who was far too appealing for my own good. He'd use me up and spit me out, and I'd be left with memories I wasn't sure I could handle.

I pushed out a breath, gathered my composure, before I dug into my small handbag and pulled out my phone so I could call for an Uber.

I had to get out of here before I completely fell prey to the man's charms.

Five minutes the app promised. Five minutes, and I'd be safely tucked away in a car that would carry me out of this fantasy world and set my feet firmly back into my reality. Where I was plain and ordinary and didn't draw the attention of movie stars who could snap their fingers and have any woman they wanted begging at their feet.

Where I lived a simple life teaching the kids I loved and didn't attend movie premiere after parties.

Where I was safe.

And safe was where I wanted to be.

Sucking in a breath, I drew open the door and stepped out into the hall dimed with shadows and the echo of the party happening at its end.

But in it, the presence was profound. Something great and intense. The breath I'd sucked in left me on a whoosh when I was suddenly pinned up against the wall by a big body.

So warm.

Overpowering.

Gorgeous.

Fingertips trailed along the slope of my neck, and my heart shuddered and shook, my pulse erratic as I looked up at the man staring down at me. "Are you okay?"

His worry took me by surprise.

But more surprising was the answer that popped up in my head.

No.

I was definitely not okay. This man had managed to knock me

from my axis. He was making me want things I would never allow myself to have.

"Why would you think I'm not?" I asked instead, caught off guard by his concern.

In a flash of that playful mischief, a smirk pulled at one side of his mouth. "Oh, I don't know…a gorgeous woman suddenly runs into the restroom to remove herself from the unwanted advances of a man. It sounds like *Ditch the Douchebag 101* to me. And that's not a label I take so kindly to."

It was all a tease wrapped up in what I was sure was true concern, those brown eyes deep and dark and intent.

I swallowed around the lump in my throat, my eyes blinking through the cloud of confused attraction. "You make my head spin," I answered in all honesty.

He backed me up farther, my body plastered to the wall, his hot as hell body pressed against me.

My thighs shook when I felt his length pleading at my belly, heavy and hard and more prominent than any wild fantasy I could have conjured.

Desire surged, and I had the overwhelming urge to press my hands to his chest, to his cock, to let them explore and trace and discover.

He dipped his head, his mouth an inch from mine. Hovering. Wavering. His lips a mere breath away from becoming a kiss.

His voice dropped so low, it shook through me like a tremor. "And what I want is to make your body sing."

"I don't do this," I whispered, feeling everything caving in around me. My willpower and self-control.

"Don't do what?" he asked even lower.

His lips just brushed mine when he spoke.

Fire.

Trembling, I forced out the words. "One night."

It was the truth. I'd never just fallen into a man's bed. Had never allowed a complete stranger to touch me.

But maybe that was the most dangerous thing about Paxton Myles. He didn't feel like a stranger. His face so familiar, his over-the-top world shoved in our faces in magazines and movies and the tabloids.

The fantasy.

Paxton growled, his big hands cradling me at the sides of my neck. "Who said anything about one night?"

I almost released the incredulous laugh bottled in my chest. But I was too busy getting lost in his gaze to chastise him for alluding to things we both knew would be nothing less than a lie.

Because we both knew exactly what this was.

Those eyes searched my face, and his tongue darted out, swiping across his full bottom lip.

My lips parted on a sigh. There was nothing I could do to stop it from happening.

Nothing I could do to stop his kiss when his mouth fell against mine.

Because I didn't want to. Didn't want to resist.

His lips were soft at first, teasing caresses that sent a rush of chills scattering through my insides. He flicked my bottom lip with his tongue. Warm and soft and wet.

I opened to him, let him draw me closer as he kissed me deeper. Our tongues were a tangle of exploration.

And want.

Hot.

Unrelenting.

Ruthless.

He took, and I so willingly gave.

My phone rang in my purse, jarring us out of the rapture.

He jerked back.

His expression was enough to steal my breath.

The man was so insanely gorgeous.

Larger than life.

Adored by millions.

And he was looking at me in awe.

In lust.

As if I was the only thing he could see.

"My Uber is here." The words were clogged with my own desire as I forced them out.

He gripped me tighter, his words a rasp. "Come home with

me."

A weighted moment spun around us.

My indecision snagged and snarled with the abounding lust.

"Okay."

Wait, what?

I had to be insane.

A needy sound rumbled up his throat, and he dipped down, kissed me again.

This time hard and quick.

Possessive.

With a promise.

Then my hand was back in his. "This way," he said.

He hauled me down the hall in the opposite direction of the party. The man clearly knew his way around as he quietly latched open a door and slipped us into the silence of a large storage room.

A gasp shot from me when he suddenly spun me around and pressed my bottom up against a table, his kiss verging on mad as he searched me in the dark, hands slipping down my sides and grazing across my breasts.

My stomach flipped and my heart rate kicked.

His touch elicited a moan from deep within me.

So easily.

"Oh, the things I'm going to do to you," he whispered in the dark. Then, just as fast, he was dragging me deeper into the room and ducking us out through a back door and into the Hollywood night.

Cool air brushed my overheated skin, and those anxious nerves zipped through my veins, my breaths short and ragged as he snuck us around the building, careful to keep us concealed in the shadows.

He glanced around, checking that we were in the clear, before he tightened his hold on my hand and rushed us toward a limo.

He yanked open the door. "In."

I didn't hesitate. I just jumped inside, and he was sliding in beside me with a flirty smirk on his face as he slammed it shut behind us.

He lowered the privacy glass. "My house," he threw out like an order before he closed it.

He cut his gaze toward me where I sat pinned against the far seat, squirming beneath the intensity.

His expression?

This time his expression was predatory.

He shifted on the long leather seat, crouching down on his knees where he moved to plant both hands on either side of my hips. "Hang on tight, Kaylee Rose."

At his words, desire throbbed between my thighs.

His eyes darkened with lust.

Because we both knew it.

What I was giving myself over to.

What I was surrendering.

Giving what this beautiful man was all too willing to take.

One. Wild. Night.

six

Paxton

We weave through the busy downtown streets and out of Hollywood toward my home in the Hollywood Hills. If only my driver would hurry the fuck up. With her fingers still laced through mine, Kaylee shifts nervously in the seat next to me. I can feel her anxiety and smell her desire.

"Would you like a drink?" I ask as I reach for the bottle of whiskey I had just poured from a few short hours ago.

"Champagne would be nice," she says softly. Kaylee's eyes flit around the back of the limo, taking in all the lights and knobs, while I get her a drink. "Do you always have a driver?" she asks, looking out the window.

I pause, wondering if she's serious. When she turns back to me and her innocent blue eyes meet mine, I know she is.

"No, Kaylee." I tilt her champagne glass as I carefully pour the bubbly. "Only for special occasions. I typically drive myself everywhere I need to go."

Her eyes twinkle under the lights, and her lips twist into a smile.

"I'm a normal guy. I do my own laundry and grocery shopping. I even open my own mail." I wink at her and hand her the glass of champagne.

I can see her visibly relax, and she settles into the soft leather seat. Her voice is gentle and smooth. "It's so beautiful up here," she says, her eyes fixed out the window at the winding streets we're climbing.

Most of the houses in the Hills have been bought and renovated or torn down and rebuilt into sprawling estates. The city lights of Los Angeles can be seen for miles up here, making the view priceless—one of the reasons I bought my house here in the Hills and not near the beach.

"It is," I reply. "It's my favorite part of the city."

"I can see why," she sighs, taking another sip of champagne. The limo slows, and I lower the privacy glass to give the driver the gate code so he can pull into my drive.

"Is this your house?" Her eyes widen as we pull into the drive way.

"It is."

She nods her head and smiles as we pull up the long drive.

"Not what you expected?" I ask her, and she turns to me.

"Not at all." She shakes her head a little. "It's stunning, but it's…" She purses her lips and scrunches her brows together. "I don't know, it's so normal looking."

I let out a laugh at her observation. I had this four-thousand square foot ranch-style home built a year ago. The outside is very understated to say the least, a single-story, modern ranch-style home…one you could see in any neighborhood in America. However, the inside is where the goods are.

"I like it," she says, not sure if she's talking to herself or me. As the limo stops on the large circular drive, the driver opens the back door, and I slide out first. I wait for Kaylee to appear, and I reach for her hand, helping her out.

Sliding my hand into hers and, with a wave, I send the driver on his way.

Just inside the front door, Kaylee kicks off her heels and literally moans in relief when her feet hit the floor. "I've been wanting to do that all night," she says, wiggling her toes. Her head is tipped back, and her eyes are closed as she relaxes.

Without a second thought, my hands find her soft cheeks, and

I pull her to me, pressing my lips to hers. Soft and sweet, she tastes like everything I imagined she would. "And I've been waiting to do that again."

She hums against my lips as I deepen our kiss. Our connection is palpable.

"Pax," she mumbles as I walk her backward down the hallway. Every inch of my body is aching to touch hers. I feel like a dick for not even offering to give her a tour of my place or offer her a bite to eat. But I cannot wait another second to get my hands on Kaylee.

"Mmhmm," I respond.

"Are you sure you want to do this?"

"More sure than I've ever been about anything in my life."

"Why me?" She stops us dead in our tracks. We stand in the dark hallway just outside my bedroom.

"Because when something you didn't realize you were looking for falls into your lap, literally..."—I chuckle—"...and it feels, right? You don't let it go."

"Right?" she questions.

"Yeah. I can't explain it." I shrug. "It just feels right."

She presses her hands to my chest and over my shoulders, pushing my tuxedo jacket off my shoulders and down my arms, letting it fall to a pile at my feet.

"Don't move," she says quietly, tugging on my bowtie and tossing it to the floor with the jacket. My cock is rock hard and pressing against my pants, begging for release.

"Kaylee," I begin to warn her. When her palm brushes against the front of my cock, it instantly silences me. She can see her effect on me and plays into it. Her fingers work quickly as she yanks my tuxedo shirt from my pants and unbuttons it, disposing of the crisp white shirt on the floor alongside my jacket and tie.

"My turn." I stop her, pinning her against the wall with my hips. Two can play this game. Only she pushes back—hard—and shoves me against the opposite wall.

"No. If we're doing this, I'm calling the shots."

Fucking bossy little minx.

Every ounce of self-control I had is gone. One hand pressed

firmly on my chest to hold me in place, she uses the other to unfasten the belt and button on my pants.

"Kaylee," I warn her again when her fingers brush against my dick.

"Pax," she warns back as she slips her hand inside my boxer briefs grasping me.

"Jesus," I hiss, and she giggles. She actually laughs.

She urges my pants off my hips and down my legs, pulling the boxer briefs down with them. She's has me totally exposed and hasn't let me even touch her yet.

"Kaylee," I warn, this time more aggressively.

She pauses, but only momentarily. "Two more minutes. Just give me two minutes. I promise, it'll be worth it."

Before I even have a chance to reply, she's dropped to her knees, dragging her hands down my stomach along with her. Her fingernails igniting a trail of goose bumps as they travel even farther, where she finally cups my balls in the palm of her hand.

Suddenly, warm lips wrap around the head of my cock, and nothing can stop the low growl that leaves my mouth when her tongue brushes against my sensitive skin. I reach down to lift her chin gently. I want to see Kaylee's blue eyes as she licks and sucks my cock. There is nothing sexier than a woman on her knees with my cock in her mouth. Instinctively, both hands reach for her head, finding the long strands of her blonde hair and I twist the silky strands through my fingers.

As good as this fucking feels, it's my turn to call the shots—it's my turn to taunt, and touch, and taste. In one swift movement, my cock is out of her mouth, and my hands pull her back up to standing.

"Turn around," I hiss into her ear as I spin her, pressing her chest to the wall. I can hear her rapid breaths and feel her heart pounding against her ribs.

My fingers work the long zipper of her dress where the black fabric falls to a pile at her feet.

"This way." I guide her carefully from behind down the hallway to my bedroom. Her bare feet slap against the travertine tile until we come to a sudden stop when her knees hit the edge of my bed.

"Hands and knees." I push her forward onto the plush bed. She inhales sharply but complies.

Good girl, I think to myself with a smile.

I turn on a small lamp that allows just enough light into the room for me to see Kaylee, but not enough to make it feel intrusive.

She's all tan skin and black lace in the middle of my bed, with big blue eyes watching me carefully.

"Kaylee, Kaylee, Kaylee." I shake my head as I inspect every inch of her on display. Running my hand over the curve of her perfect ass, I make sure to rub the small satin patch that hides the very thing I can't wait to get my lips, my tongue, and my cock on.

She gasps and thrusts as my fingers find her ready and wet. I tsk openly. "Someone is certainly ready, isn't she?" I yank one of her feet out from underneath her, causing her to fall gently to her stomach.

"Roll over," I hiss, and she does. Her blue eyes watch me intently, waiting for my next move.

"Knees up," I order her. She hesitates, but once again complies. I position myself at the end of the bed, between her knees. Her perfect tits lay across her chest covered in black lace, allowing me just the slightest peek of her pink nipples underneath.

Reaching forward, I pull the cups of her bra down. Her chest rises and falls quickly with each breath. "Look at you," I tell her as I roll one of her pink nipples between my thumb and forefinger. "So fucking beautiful, Kaylee."

My fingers follow the smooth skin of her breasts, down to her stomach, stopping at the edge of her lace panties.

She pulls her lips between her teeth and arches her back, knowing exactly what I want. Lifting her bottom, she makes it all too easy to remove her panties—the only thing that was keeping me from devouring her.

Everything about her is beautiful and has me wanting her. I want to know this woman inside and out. The nervous look in her eyes, the vulnerability written across her face…and the way her body reacts to me, tells me she's scared, but she's trusting me.

Everything about her is perfect.

Not Hollywood perfect, but the kind of perfect a man really likes. Not cosmetically enhanced perfect. But the kind of perfect that tells me everything about her is real. Every curve, every lean muscle, every scar is one-hundred percent, Kaylee.

My hands grip her hips, pulling her closer to the edge of the bed. Her knees falling apart, inviting me to touch her. My fingers find her warm and wet. She inhales sharply as my fingers touch her sensitive flesh. Her clit throbs under my touch and little moans escape her as I roll it between my fingers.

The way her body reacts to my touch drives me wild. My cock aches as I take my time exploring her. Sliding one finger and then another inside her tells me everything I need to know—she's as ready as I am. Fuck. She's tight and wet and I want to take her right now.

"Pax," she mumbles as she twists her fingers into the comforter of my bed as I hit that spot I knew she'd love.

"Feel good, sweet girl?" I ask, moving my fingers slowly in and out of her. My thumb rolls back and forth over her clit as she gasps for breath. She nods her head frantically and lifts her hips to meet my fingers as they work her over. She exhales loudly as I pull my fingers from her and pull a condom from my bedside drawer. Rolling the thin sheath over my cock, I position myself at her center doing everything to not plunge right into her.

"Look at me, Kaylee," I instruct her.

Her blue eyes meet mine, full of lust.

"I want to see your eyes when I fill you," I say quietly as I push inside her slowly. Her eyes flutter closed and back open as I slide into her. Her chest rises and falls with every inch until I've gone as deep as I can.

A small smile tugs at one corner of her lips as I begin to slowly move. "Gonna make you come so hard, Kaylee," I mutter as I push in and out of her. Her thighs shake and her head falls back farther with every thrust.

I hold her knees apart and revel in the sight of where we connect. Her soft pink flesh, wet with her arousal, accepting me. My body fights, torn between wanting to fuck her like a wild animal, and taking my time with her—devouring her for hours.

Suddenly, her foot to my chest stops me, and a smirk tugs at the corner of her mouth. "Lay down," she says, catching me off guard.

"Nope. Nuh uh. This is all me. I'm calling the shots now."

"Just lay down," she says and wiggles to the center of the bed, breaking our connection. I sigh, but do as I'm told, lying down next to her. She rolls over, swinging a leg over me so that she's now straddling me. Using her fingertips on my chest to balance herself, she wastes no time...sliding onto me. A perfect fit. Nice and tight.

Fuck. Oh Jesus, fuck.

My fingers find the soft curve of her hips where I hold onto her for dear life. I can make out the smirk on her face as she begins to ride me slow and methodic.

"Jesus, woman," I hiss as she begins moving faster. Reaching down between us, she squeezes the base of my cock and all I see are fireworks. Fireworks and Kaylee's perfect tits bouncing in my face. Leaning forward, I'm barely able to pull one of her taut nipples into my mouth, causing her to gasp loudly as I bite.

Only fair.

I don't know how we manage to spend the next hour devouring each other, but we do. On the bed, the floor, and against the wall, when we both finally climax, we fall into an exhausted knot of twisted limbs onto my bed.

Kaylee's head is curled up under my chin, and I'm able to make out the steady sound of her breaths telling me she's fast asleep. Only then do I finally close my eyes, pulling her tightly to me. What was supposed to be one wild night, could certainly be so much more.

seven

Kaylee

I barely cracked open an eye. Faint hues of sunlight streaked in from the window, prodding me from sleep I didn't want to be roused from.

I was too comfortable.

Too cozy.

Too warm.

A bit disoriented, I tried to stretch out my body.

My *sore* body that was wrapped up by a body so much bigger than mine, eclipsed where it was caged.

What the hell?

My head popped up two inches, considering I was pinned and couldn't rise any higher.

Eyes widening, they wandered, trying to process my surroundings.

The expansive, masculine room.

A room with a view so dramatic it stole what little breath I had left.

But what was freaking me the hell out was the bed that was not my own.

And the man…

Oh. God.

The man who was spooning me from behind.

Spooning. Me.

In what crazy world did that happen?

My heart rate kicked up as memories of last night came barreling in.

Pinned against the wall.

Back arched as I begged.

A hot, hot mouth on my breast.

His throbbing cock in my hand.

Paxton Myles buried deep inside of me.

Stealing my breath.

Stealing my sanity.

Pulling the most mind-blowing pleasure from my body. Again and again.

Chills spread across my bare skin.

Never before had I experienced a night quite like it. The few boyfriends I'd had hadn't even come close. Couldn't have.

That would be an impossibility.

No doubt, this Hollywood god had ruined me for all men.

He'd given me a taste of fantasy when I knew I had to be stepping back into my reality.

The problem was, I wanted to stay there for a little while longer, which was exactly why I needed to get the hell out of there.

Holding my breath, I pried myself out from under his massive arm, careful not to wake him.

He rolled all the way onto his stomach, his ridiculously handsome face peeking out from the pillow, the curve of those full, red lips enough to send those butterflies in my body into a tailspin.

Flitting and fluttering.

My mouth watered as my gaze traced down, memorizing the strength of his wide shoulders and the defined cut of his slim waist.

A satiny sheet was pulled to above his hips.

But I knew firsthand what was hidden underneath.

The stark beauty of pure man.

Bold and big and powerful.

A shudder rolled through my senses, tingles ushered in by his phantom touch.

I shouldn't have been surprised. Not after last night. Only Paxton Myles could bring another rush of pleasure from me while he was fast asleep.

I fought an affectionate smile as I looked down at him once more. Warmth welled in my chest as I tucked the memories inside. I would never forget the miraculous night this incredible man had offered me.

My Hollywood crush.

My free card.

Well, I guess that was that.

I'd cashed it in.

I allowed myself one last glance, a barely-there caress of my fingertips across those lips that last night had devoured every inch of my body, before I slipped from his bed.

Silently, I tiptoed across the cool, travertine floors, gathered my lingerie and wadded it at my chest as I stole out the crack in the door. I moved a little bit faster as soon as I hit the hall, even quicker as I slinked into my dress where it'd been abandoned on the floor.

I shoved my balled-up bra and panties into my clutch.

Classy.

I dug my phone out of my clutch, the battery low, but it at least had enough juice for me to hail an Uber.

Thank God.

Snatching my heels from the floor, I unlatched the front door lock, the straps of my heels wound through my fingers and swinging from one hand.

Harsh sunlight glared down, and I squinted against the intrusion. In the clarity of day, things became so much more obvious.

My disheveled appearance. The hair I was rockin' screamed I'd just spent the entire night being completely and utterly ravaged. Smeared make-up.

I had to look like a train wreck.

My stomach twisted at the realization.

I was doing a straight up walk of shame.

Never before had I felt so exposed or on display.

Pulling in a stealing breath, I lifted my chin and marched down the long drive.

It was time to leave this night behind.

Toss a padlock on this sucker and let the weeds grow up around it.

Like a beautiful old house with the windows boarded up.

Buried but never forgotten.

Just distant memories that could never be reclaimed.

Ones that only I would ever know.

Because girls like me didn't do these types of reckless things.

Like climb a freaking wrought-iron gate wearing this damned dress to even get out of the compound.

I was betting that was pretty.

I scoffed. Nothing but a poster child for elegance and sophistication.

Yeah right.

I dropped down on the other side.

As soon as I saw the small black sedan slow, looking for me, I all but ran for it.

Because I couldn't stand to think of what I looked like right then for a second longer. I ducked into the backseat and breathed out a relieved breath.

The car flipped a U in the middle of the road, and I chanced looking back over my shoulder.

The tiniest flash of sadness swept through my senses.

No man had ever affected me the way Paxton Myles had. He had ruined me in the best of ways. I honestly doubted another could compare.

And there was just something about him...something more than that megawatt smile and his mind-blowing kisses.

But that was the thing about fantasies. You could only live in them for a little while.

Just before we rounded the curve, I whispered a silent goodbye to my *one wild night*.

I blew out a relieved breath and sagged against the inside of my front door, reaching back to lock it behind me. I tossed my keys to the small bowl on the entryway table, tossed my clutch behind, and plugged in my dead phone to recharge.

Forty-five minutes and an $80.00 fare later, I was home free.

My townhouse was small, and I walked through the cozy living room with the overstuffed couch and messy coffee table, the walls lined with books and pictures and knickknacks, as I made my way into my room and to my tiny en suite bathroom that wasn't much larger than a closet.

Swanky, I know.

I turned on the shower full blast, relishing a calming breath as steam began to billow into the small room.

First order of business was ridding myself of the dress.

It pooled at my feet, and I kicked it aside where it was left in a heaped-up ball. I only felt the teeniest twinge of guilt for completely ruining Elle's dress. One I could do without knowing the price tag of.

I hadn't decided if she'd ruined my night or completely made it. I still hadn't settled on whether to chew her out for not showing or to sing her praises.

I was sure what happened last night wouldn't have happened had she been there.

I stepped into the warm spray. A tiny moan rolled up my throat as the pounding water began to ease my tight muscles, my hips perfectly sore from where Paxton had gripped them tight.

An ache of pure satisfaction throbbed between my thighs. An ache I secretly prayed would never go away.

I washed and rinsed, slowly dried and applied lotion, all the while allowing myself to savor the memories spinning through my head.

I bit my lip, fighting a blush when I thought of all the things we'd done. My face was flushed when I looked in the mirror, and I was betting it had zero to do with the hot shower I'd just stepped from and rather the unforgettable experience from last night.

Life was little more than a gathering of memories.

These were memories I was never going to let go of.

I slipped into a cozy pair of shorts and a tee, figuring after last night I was due a lazy day. I headed into the kitchen, made a piece of toast, and fiddled with my Keurig for a cup of coffee.

Once it was properly doused with sugar and creamer, I took a sip and bit into my toast, enjoying them both as I wandered back to the entryway and fired back up my phone.

Ding.

Ding.

Ding.

I frowned.

I had like a gazillion messages. Before I had a chance to check any of them, my phone began to ring.

Elle's picture and name lit up the faceplate.

A grin split my mouth.

I swallowed around the toast I was chewing, quick to answer the phone, my tone playful and light.

Apparently, it hadn't taken me all that much to decide which side I'd landed on.

I was thankful.

Thankful I got the experience.

The memories.

I wouldn't trade them for anything.

"Hey, hooker," I said, "You better have a good explanation for last night. For real…all the details, and they'd better be good."

Knowing Elle, it would be *all kinds of good.*

Silence echoed from the other end, and then Elle's voice came on, almost incredulous. "You're seriously calling me hooker right now?"

I paused. Frowned. Confused. "What?"

"Hello pot calling the kettle black. Who are you and what did you do with my best friend?"

A twist of unease tightened in my chest. "What are you talking about?"

"Tell me you didn't sleep with Paxton Myles last night."

I gasped, my head shaking as I took a step back. "How…how…?"

"Oh, God." The words were low, coated with worry. "Kay…you don't know."

That twist of unease grew into a cyclone of anxiety. "You're freaking me out. Tell me what you're talking about."

Elle hesitated, then said, "I'll be right over."

"Elle," I begged.

The line went dead.

I glanced at my phone. I had a ton of missed calls from my mom and my sister, not to mention the slew of texts from the two of them. That anxiety churned and twisted when I saw I'd also missed a bunch texts from a few of my co-workers and acquaintances from the school where I worked.

People I rarely, if ever, spoke to outside of school.

Dread balled at the base of my throat, and I shuffled into my living room. The sheer drapes pulled across the arcadia door glowed like fire. It cast the rest of the room in warm blues and bright shadows.

I leaned over the back of the couch and reached for the remote I'd left sitting on the seat cushion. My hands were shaking like crazy when I clicked on the TV that had been set to mute. Pointing the remote, I changed the channel, because even though I didn't want to believe it, I knew.

I knew.

Still, I wasn't prepared.

I wasn't prepared in the least.

There were pictures.

Pictures in a little square box that kept popping up above the reporter's head. Playing out on a reel. Paxton on the red carpet, looking like a million bucks as he flashed that megawatt smile. Another of him with his friend Philip.

But it was the ones of me that hooked my breath on the lump at the base of my throat.

The first was one of me walking the red carpet, looking so out of place, like a timid, plain mouse who'd lost her way. The second was a fuzzy shot taken in the hall outside the women's restroom in the hotel, my back pressed to the wall where Paxton Myles' big body concealed mine.

The reporter's mouth moved a million miles a minute as he waved his hands in excitement, even though I couldn't hear what he said.

Even if the volume had been turned up, I'm still not sure I would have heard. Because a low buzz started to hum in my ears, obliterating all senses except for what my eyes were forced to see.

Because the first two weren't what brought on the rush of horror.

No.

It was the ones of me outside Paxton's Hollywood Hills mansion from this morning. Shots of me as I strode down the drive through the slots of the wrought iron fence, though they somehow made me appear as if I was limping, my shoulders slack with shame.

There were more of me climbing up and jumping over the gate.

They'd obviously been snatched from a distance. The pictures were cropped to bring me nearer and were a little grainy.

But that didn't matter.

Because they were so utterly clear.

My hair was even worse than I'd imagined, a matted mess on one side and poofed up on the other, my dress twisted and wrinkled, black mascara smeared around my eyes.

Barefoot.

For some reason, that seemed the worst.

Nausea swelled.

I didn't know why, but there was something about it that made me look used up. Cheap and trashy.

I glanced back where my heels had been abandoned on the floor just inside my front door, toppled in a messy pile.

Why the hell didn't I put on those damned shoes?

What had I done?

My phone rang again.

Almost numb, I lifted it to see who was calling. My mother's sweet face was smiling back at me.

Without a doubt, she wasn't smiling right now.

What had I done?

Knees feeling wobbly and weak, I mindlessly moved around to

the front of the couch and sank down onto the cushions. In horror, I sat there and watched in silence as the same thing played out over and over again on my television, different reporters piping in, giving their own salacious opinion.

My private life nothing less than entertainment.

What had I done?

I dropped my face into my hands. I didn't even realize I was crying until my shoulders started to heave up and down.

How much time had passed before there was banging on my door, I didn't know, but I jolted with the impatient rattle of the knob, a key shoved into the lock.

The door flew open and knocked into the wall.

Warily, I looked that way over the back of the couch.

Elle stood there in all her glory, holding a big paper sack to her chest, my best friend a blur where I watched her through bleary eyes.

"Holy shit, Kay Kay. What have I always said? If you're going to do it, do it big. You sure as hell knocked it out of the park."

Elle emerged from my small kitchen wielding two glasses of red wine. She passed one to me. "To taking life by the balls and making it your bitch."

My laugh was part incredulous, part scoff. "Pretty sure life's making me its bitch right about now."

"Pssh." Elle waved the thought off and curled her legs up underneath her where she sat down next to me on the couch. She took a sip of her wine, narrowing her brown eyes as she searched my expression. "Don't tell me last night wasn't amazing. I mean, we're talking Paxton Myles here. One of the most sought-after bachelors in all of Hollywood. And you snagged him."

I lifted a brow. "Shagged, not snagged. He doesn't belong to me."

Elle almost spit out a mouthful of wine. She slammed her hand over her mouth to hold it in, laughing so hard I couldn't help but laugh a little bit, too. She finally got the wine down, her words rambling out on jutted spurts of laughter. "Oh my God…did you actually just say shagged?"

I shrugged. "What?"

"It's not 1950."

I pointed at the TV that was, surprise, surprise, once again talking about Paxton and my *illicit affair.* "They sure seem to think so." I scowled with a pout. "You'd think I stole Paxton's virginity."

Elle howled. "Yeah right. That boy has been around the block more times than I can count."

Ouch. I chose to ignore the insinuation.

Elle gestured to the TV. "But you know how these assholes are going to play it… *no name girl tries to sink her greedy claws into Hollywood heartthrob.*" She touched her hand over her heart, the words dripping   sarcasm.
"Oh, the scandal. The vultures are going to eat that one up."

I cringed.

Vultures.

Just like Paxton had warned.

I guessed he'd been right all along.

Elle winced when she realized what she'd said. "Sorry. You know that's not what I think."

"I know that. But you know that's what everyone else is going to think."

She gave me a shrug and a lascivious grin. "Who cares what everyone else thinks? You got to *shag* Paxton Myles." With a grin playing all over her mouth, she poked me in the side. "Tell me how it was…are the rumors true? Heard the boy is packed and he's a king in the sack."

I could feel the redness crawl to my cheeks. I shook my head, diverting. "Eww…Elle…so crass. And why don't you tell me where you were last night?"

She scoffed. "Oh, no. You're not getting out of this one. My pretty much prude of a best friend spent all last night doing all kinds of dirty, delicious deeds with *the* Paxton Myles. You can't go and hook up with one of the hottest guys on the planet and not dish the details. That's like…best friend foul number one. Don't go and break my heart."

More redness.

She prodded me again. "Tell me."

"Okay, okay…he was…"

"Yes…?" she drew out.

I slanted my attention her direction, and my voice went soft. "He owned me, Elle."

Elle's expression did the same, and she tilted her head as she touched my hand. "Hey…are you okay? I know this has to be a lot for you. You're not exactly the love 'em and leave 'em type. I'm honestly kind of shocked."

Yeah.

So was I.

I dropped my gaze to watch the deep red liquid swirl in my wine glass. "I'll be fine. It was just…it was supposed to be one night. Between him and me. Private. It was a big deal to me, and now the entire world is talking about it like it's entertainment. It's…embarrassing."

Wrong.

Humiliating.

Mortifying.

I wanted to crawl into a hole and hide.

And people needed to learn to mind their own damned business.

She patted my knee. "It'll blow over, Kay Kay. You'll see. Give it a couple days and no one will even remember it. Paxton will be back to being a player, and you'll be back to being the old schoolmarm who never sees any action."

She winked at me, and I slugged at her arm. "That's not nice."

She rubbed her arm. "And that hurt."

"Good."

My phone lit up with another call from my mother, and I cringed as I held it in my hand, letting it ring until it went to voicemail.

Elle inclined her head toward it. "Seriously, Kaylee…give it a couple of days. It'll all be good. I promise."

eight
Paxton

The morning sun assaults me, and I barely manage to crack an eye open before the pounding in my head starts. A pleasureful ache had settled into my muscles, surely from the hours of wild sex Kaylee and I indulged in just hours ago.

I can still smell her on my skin and selfishly I need more.

Want more.

With a pillow over my face, I extend an arm to pull her closer, wanting to brush my fingers across her soft, fair skin...wanting to pull her underneath me for another go at it this morning.

Morning sex.

The sure-fire way to cure a hangover.

I reach farther across the bed, looking for her, and come up empty handed. Flinging the pillow from my face, I sit up quickly, noticing my abs are deliciously tender from having my way with Kaylee last night.

I quietly listen for any sign of Kaylee. I listen for the shower, but it isn't running, and I don't hear movement from the kitchen.

I search for her clothes on the floor, or her phone on the nightstand, and come up with nothing—she's gone. Her absence is immediately noticeable. Disappointment washes over me at the thought of her leaving—without a goodbye—without even a phone number.

It's then I hear the dull buzz of a phone. Instead of bothering to find it, I throw myself back on the bed and cover my face with the pillow again, ignoring it. I'm not ready to deal with reality when all I want to do is be lost in Kaylee.

Closing my eyes, I succumb to the memories of Kaylee last night...on top of me, under me, and in front of me. On all fours, on her back, and with her legs wrapped tightly around me.

We tried damn near every position and every single one of them was my favorite—or maybe it was just her. She made me feel things I've never felt before—and I fucking loved it. I need more of it. Sex with Kaylee is like a drug. I'm dying for my next fix.

My mouth waters as I remember how she tasted.

That neck.

Those breasts.

Her pussy.

I'll never forget how my tongue explored every inch of her soft, sweet body. My skin tingles as I remember how my fingers touched every inch of her.

I try to doze off, shrugging off the disappointment her absence has left, but the damn buzzing of my phone won't let me. It's when the doorbell rings over and over that I force myself out of bed. Twisting a sheet around my waist, I shuffle down the hallway to the door.

"Hold on," I mumble as I approach. Through the peephole, I can see the stick straight dark hair and bright red lips that can only belong to Kendall. *Fuck.*

"Morning, Kendall!" I smile as I open the door and step back to let her in. I run my hands through my wild hair and wait for her reaction.

She steps inside, her long legs covered in leather pants, and an oversized sheer white shirt covers her tan skin. An arm full of bangle bracelets make all kinds of fucking annoying racket as her heels click on the floor, causing my head to pound even harder.

With her cell phone pressed to her ear, I can hear copious amounts of yelling on the other end. She remains calm, which tells me she's dealing with another client issue.

Thank God.

But, it's when she turns toward me that I see the look in her eye. The look I've seen more than a couple times when she's bailing me out of the bullshit I drag her ass into. The look that says I'm fucking dead meat. The look that tells me I better get my shit together—and fast.

Finally pulling her phone from her ear, she just looks at me. I'm not sure if it's disappointment, disgust, or hatred. It's a look I've seen all too often from her, though, and I hate that look.

"What in the ever-loving fuck were you thinking?" she barks at me as she shoves her phone into her back pocket.

I sigh exaggeratedly. "What, Kendall? I'm a grown man. I can bring a woman home if I want too." I don't know how Kendall even keeps me as a client. I swear, this is my excuse every time. I mean, what am I supposed to say? I shouldn't have to have an excuse to get laid every now and then. A man has needs.

Her eyes are so narrow I can barely make out the color of her irises. "Have you even turned on the television, Pax?" She points to the large television that sits on the wall in my den. "Whatever her name is, was seen crawling over your fence this morning. They have pictures of her, Pax, climbing…over…your…fence…in a dress. Who is she?" Her voice is high-pitched and fast. She wants answers, and my brain is moving at the speed of a snail in molasses right now.

"Calm the fuck down," I tell her and walk toward the den where I throw myself onto the oversized sectional, reaching for the remote control. Pushing a few buttons, the TV roars to life and, sure as shit, there is Kaylee…black dress, bare feet, and wild hair, scaling my gates. I try to crack a smile as I see her struggle to get over. God, she's beautiful.

"Who. Is. She. Pax?" Kendall asks bitterly, following me into the room. I don't even know how to answer all the questions she's asking me, nor does she deserve an answer. Kaylee isn't her business. She slams her hand down on the sofa table to get my attention.

"Who is she? How did you meet her? Are you dating? How do

you know her?" She pulls her phone from her pocket as it vibrates wildly in her hand. "Give me some goddamn answers, Pax! I have every fucking media outlet in the United States and half of them from Europe blowing up my phone. They want a statement. They want to know if America's most eligible bachelor is off the market, and I don't even know this bitch's name!" she yells at me. "And for the love of God, put some fucking clothes on."

She rolls her eyes at me and steps away to take the call that's coming in.

I don't care about clothes right now. All I care about is right there on my television set. Kaylee. Her picture scrolling across the television.

Mystery woman.

Escort.

Who is she?

My stomach flips when I see a breaking news banner begin flashing before my eyes.

Mystery solved! Kaylee Burton. Kindergarten teacher, it reads.

They know who she is. The sudden urge to protect Kaylee from this mess takes over. She didn't want this life. She didn't ask for this. My selfish ass, wanting her—needing her—brought her into this.

"Fuck!" I yell, jumping from the couch, hurrying down the hall to my bedroom in search of my phone. Tossing clothes left and right, I finally find my pants. Reaching into the pocket, I find my phone and a slew of texts and calls from Kendall, Philip, and even my sister.

I scroll through my contacts, hoping like hell I was gentleman enough to at least get Kaylee's contact information before sticking my dick in her—but nope.

"Fuck!" I yell again in frustration. It's about all I can conjure up right now. Slamming my bedroom door closed, I drop the sheet I have tied around my waist and head to the shower. Some hot water and peace and quiet is exactly what I need to figure out what in the hell I need to do.

Kendall can't save me from this one—hell, I don't want her too. I don't need saving, I need to find Kaylee. I need to make this right. I step into the glass encased shower, allowing the steam to fill my lungs and the hot water to prick my skin.

Water stings the light scratches on my back from Kaylee and every muscle is gloriously sore from last night's marathon of sex. No woman has ever had me tied up in knots like this, and I almost chuckle as I think about how one wild night turned into one fucking nightmare.

nine
Kaylee

I didn't sleep.

How could I?

Exhaustion warred with the paranoia, a dueling duo that churned in the pit of my stomach. Clutching the steering wheel, I peered out at the small private school in front of me from where I was parked in the staff lot.

You can do this.

It was the same pep talk I'd been giving myself since I'd finally dragged myself from the fitful tossing of my bed and into the shower.

Yesterday I'd decided to ignore all the calls and texts that had come in from my co-workers, demanding to know what happened.

I figured it was all just morbid curiosity, anyway. Fodder for water cooler gossip. None of their business. So, when my phone continued to ding and ring throughout the day, I'd switched it off and opted for a day on the couch with my best friend and a bottle of wine.

Okay, two.

Could anyone blame me?

Of course, my own morbid curiosity had set in the second Elle had left me for the night with the promise it would blow over. Quick to be forgotten. But as soon as the quiet had set in, all the implications had come barreling back. The things the reporters had said and the insinuations they had made.

So, what did I do? Because I'm just that much of a masochist, I went and typed #PaxtonMyles into my Twitter search.

That was the worst thing I could have done.

The cruel, vicious things complete strangers had said about me had haunted me all night. You could call it jealousy. The rabid fangirls who had so many nasty things to say about me.

Just mean.

Not to mention hypocritical.

Because there was no doubt in my mind every single one of them would have jumped at the chance to kick me out of that spot.

I took one last glance in the rear-view mirror.

And cringed.

This morning, I had to look worse off than the pictures had proclaimed when I'd been hopping Paxton's gate.

Nothing I could do about it now, and I needed to get into my classroom to get things set up for the beginning of the week.

Sucking in a deep breath, I grabbed my bag and stepped out into the warm day, the California sun bright and way cheerier than I felt. I tucked my head and stared at my feet as I made a beeline for my classroom.

I'd give it a good go to just hide until all of this blew over.

I gasped when the large figure stepped out in front of me, shadow eclipsing me, my body coming to a jilted stop the flash of a second before I'd have barreled right into him.

Steven Washington.

My boss.

The headmaster of Kensington Palisades.

That war that was going on in my stomach? It plummeted right to the ground.

Swallowing around the huge knot in my throat, I warily glanced up. His face was tight and grim, his stance harsh.

"Ms. Burton, would you please come with me to my office."

I hesitated, stuttered over the words. "Uh...I need to get to my classroom to get things—"

"It wasn't a question, Ms. Burton."

He didn't wait for me to answer. He spun on his heel without further word and headed toward the front of the building. He moved through the side door and into his big office filled with heavy dark brown leather chairs and even darker furniture.

He gestured to a chair facing his desk as he sank into his leather office rocker. "Have a seat."

Unsteadily, I lowered myself to the seat, sitting just on the edge, clutching my bag to my chest. I couldn't even meet his eye.

"Ms. Burton."

He said it like a warning.

An omen.

And I just knew.

"I'm so sorry." It came out on a strained gush of apologetic air.

I could almost see him shaking his head, resigned. "You know what a wonderful job you've done for this school…"

No. No. No.

Don't say it.

"I'm so sorry. I don't know what you saw, but I can assure you—"

"And I can assure you I saw enough." Once again, he cut me off.

Panicked, I turned tactic. "What I do with my personal life doesn't reflect on my ability as a teacher."

He sighed. "See…that is where you're wrong, Ms. Burton. Kensington Palisades has a reputation to uphold as the premiere private school in the area, and…well…it seems you've gained yourself your own *reputation* this weekend."

Horror latched onto my chest, and he just continued on, "I fielded calls all weekend from concerned parents…worried about what kind of influence you are on their kindergartners. I'm sorry, but that is not the type of concern we as a school can shoulder nor overlook."

"What are you saying?" The words spilled out. Harsh and desperate.

"I'm saying we are going to have to let you go."

Devastation bottled in my chest, and I struggled for a breath. "But my kids," I pled.

"Are no longer your concern. We've called in a substitute until we can find a permanent replacement."

I blinked. Dazed. "Sir."

I could feel him shaking his head. His voice softened. "I'm sorry, Kaylee. I am. I like you, and you're a good teacher. But my bottom line is this school and its well-being. You know as well as I do how difficult these parents are to please. And with something as public as this…" he trailed off, letting the rest hang in the air.

I nodded my head.

I wasn't sure it was in acceptance, because really, I couldn't process anything.

Nothing but this nagging regret.

A quiet devastation.

"Kirk will show you to your office so you can gather your things and escort you out."

Disoriented, I nodded again, stumbled to my feet. My eyes moved to the security guard already waiting at the door.

Oh. God.

A wave of sadness hit me.

How could this be happening? My entire life, the only thing I'd ever wanted to be was a teacher, and I'd destroyed that dream with one reckless mistake.

Humiliated, I studied my feet. The pile of the carpet. The tiny fleck of paper. Anything but the pity on the old man's face who I considered my friend. I shuffled his way.

"Let's get your things, Ms. Burton," he said so quietly I could barely hear, though there was no missing the sympathy that was woven into it.

"Okay."

Kirk set a box on my desk, and I loaded it with the few things that actually belonged to me. A picture of me with my family, a few drawings the kids had done for me, my planner.

"All done," I said, offering Kirk a feeble smile that was so entirely forced I was fairly certain my face might crack with the strain of it.

That was when another rush of sadness came swooping in.

Binding to my heart.

I followed him out into the hall where children were beginning to arrive. I could feel the burn of the parents' stares, those who had shunned and shamed me because of one night.

I tried to ignore the snickers and hushed conversations that weren't so hushed that I couldn't hear.

Slut.

Gold digger.

Tramp.

Seriously, was this 1972?

Kirk led me all the way out to my car. "Take care of yourself now, Kaylee Rose. Don't let none of this get to you. You're a good girl. All of us smart ones know it, too. It'll all work out. Just wait. But I'm sure gonna miss you 'round here."

I wished he were right.

That Elle had been right.

That it'd just blow over.

Forgotten in days.

But they were so utterly wrong.

I slumped down in my car and started the engine, quick to leave the lot because I couldn't stand the stares for a second more. I drove the twenty minutes to my condo.

Halfway home, I had to send yet another call from my mother to voicemail.

Then I turned around and tortured myself with her message.

Tears streaked down my face as I listened to her words.

Kaylee Rose, call me, baby girl. Your face is all over the place and all the neighbors are calling, asking questions, looking for something else to add to the gossip. I need to know that you're okay. I'm all the way across the country, and I don't know if you're okay. Please call me.

I deleted her message, whispered into my car, "No, Mama, I'm not okay."

Because one wild night had turned into my worst nightmare.

Of course, that nightmare only got worse when I pulled up to my townhouse.

Paparazzi.

Everywhere.

Emotion knotted up everywhere. Embarrassment. Sadness. And anger.

Anger.

Suddenly, there was a whole lot of that.

How dare they take my picture without my knowing? How dare these parents take the most important thing away from me— their children? My job and my future and my career.

My joy.

How dare Paxton Myles chase me all night until I succumbed to his charms?

How dare HE?!

Somewhere deep inside I knew it was just as much my fault as it was his. I'd made the choice, and God, it'd been just about the best night I'd ever had.

But was it worth the price?

Regret pressed at my chest.

Not even close.

I ducked my head, praying the photographers would just let me be, and pulled into my spot. I didn't sit and wait or catch my breath.

I bolted out of the door with my key in my hand, ran across the parking lot, and fumbled to shove the key into the lock.

At the same second, I was surrounded. Lights flashed and questions fired. A barrage of voices pummeled me left and right.

Kaylee, can you tell me about your relationship with Paxton Myles.

Are you dating Paxton Myles, Ms. Burton?

Is it true you are an aspiring actress?

Can you comment on being released from your position at Kensington Palisades?

Kaylee.

Kaylee.

Kaylee.

It all became a buzz of horror in my ears. I finally got the door open and stumbled into the dim light inside. Gasping for a breath, I slammed the door shut behind me.

Thankfully, all the drapes were drawn over the windows to

keep out the light, not to mention the outside intrusion and speculation.

I pressed my back to the door. Trying to calm my racing heart. Trying to shove off the panic and to slow the quickly settling dread as I fully began to process what fooling around with a Hollywood god had cost me.

That gorgeous, Greek god.

The man with a wicked smile and a perfect touch.

It had cost me everything.

I dragged myself to the couch and slumped down on it, fighting the tears that burned at my eyes, wishing there was a way to drown out everything. To go back and change the decision I'd made.

But there was no escape.

Because throughout the day, the doorbell continued to ring.

Anger and frustration and sorrow burned in my blood, ramping into irritation and anxiety. My nerves shot, and my stomach in a million knots.

When it rang again, I'd had enough.

I'd had enough of the prying.

Enough of the intrusion.

With my hands balled in fists, I stomped to the front door and threw it open, a slew of profanities poised on my tongue, because I refused to cower and hide.

Then everything froze. All except for my heart that took off at a sprint.

Because standing at my door was none other than Paxton Myles.

ten
Paxton

My knuckles sting from beating on this door for the last five minutes, but I'll be damned if I'm going anywhere until she opens it. I refuse to glance over my shoulder at those heathens trying to get another shot of Kaylee with their cameras.

"Pax, can you tell us the status of your relationship with Kaylee Burton?" one reporter from a tabloid television show hollers from behind me.

"Can you confirm if she was fired from her job at Kensington Palisades as it's been reported?" another yells.

"Open the fucking door, Kaylee," I mumble to myself as I rap on the door again, this time with more force...more desperation. I lean forward, my head hanging in defeat as another reporter hollers an inaudible question from behind me.

A gush of cool air assaults me as the front door flies open and, when I lift my head, my heart stops as Kaylee stands stunned in the open doorway.

"Kay," I say quietly, hoping she'll let me in. The reporters behind us go nuts, yelling questions, while cameras click wildly, trying to get a glimpse at the both of us.

"Can I come in?"

She stares at me, tears hanging heavy in those beautiful eyes of hers. She nods and steps aside, and I carefully push her out of the way before shutting the door, leaving the world outside.

"Why are you here?" she asks, her voice breaking as she swipes at the tears that finally began to fall. I want to pull her into me and hold her, smell her. Just feel her. I need to feel her.

"Why did you leave the other morning?" I take a careful step toward her, giving her space, but closing a bit of the distance between us.

"Because I didn't want this." She flings her arm toward the door and the chaos just outside it. "Pax, I had a great time...I didn't want to leave, but you and I—" Her voice breaks, and she looks down to her feet.

"You and I what, Kaylee?"

"We're from two different worlds. I'm a kindergarten teacher...well, was a kindergarten teacher. You're a Hollywood hunk—"

I scoff at that remark.

"What? You are," she continues. "We got caught up in a wild night and the last thing I wanted was for it to affect your career...or mine."

She pushes past me, and I hate the feeling of her fleeing from me. She tosses herself down on her couch and pulls a pillow tightly into her lap. "What have we done?" she says quietly. "What have I done?" she corrects herself, placing the blame on herself.

I'll be damned if I'm going to let her do that, take the blame.

I take a deep breath and walk across her living room toward her. She looks up at me, those beautiful eyes marred in red, her cheeks splotchy from crying.

"Stand up," I order her and hold out my hand for her to take. She hesitates, dropping her eyes to my waiting hand. "Come on, Kaylee," I encourage her. She swallows hard and tosses the pillow from her lap onto the couch next to her.

With a shaky hand, she reaches for mine, her soft fingers sliding into the palm of my hand. I gently tug her closer to me when she stands up, finally getting her where she belongs—next to me. I brush my thumb across her damp cheek, wiping away any remaining tears.

"You didn't do anything wrong. I didn't do anything wrong. What we did, we did together," I start. I brush a stray piece of hair off her forehead. "What we did wasn't wrong." I pull her closer, snaking my arm around her waist. "What we did I enjoyed...and I want to do it again."

I feel her tense at my admission, and my stomach flips. What the fuck is wrong with me? I'm not an 'admit your feelings' kind of guy, and I'm pretty sure I just scared the shit out of her.

"Or, we can—"

"I'm scared," Kaylee cuts me off.

"Of what?"

"Of getting hurt. Of them." She points toward her door and the barbarians outside, trying to get the next big headline.

"Fuck them," I tell her, anger bubbling beneath the surface. I fucking hate the paparazzi, but I know how to deal with them. She doesn't. "And I can't promise you that you won't get hurt, but I can promise that I'll do everything in my power to make sure it doesn't happen."

"But—"

"Come with me, Kaylee." It's not really a question, or a demand...but it's me laying it all out there. My eyes beg her to come with me. I need her with me. I need her to give this, us, a chance. She pulls her lips between her teeth and contemplates my question.

"I'm leaving for London tonight. I have press junkets and a foreign film premiere, and I want you there with me. I want you at my side for all of this."

"What?"

"You heard me."

Confusion moves across her brow. "Why, Pax?"

"Because I like you, Kaylee. Because I like us together. Because—I don't know, something just clicks with us. It's easy, and natural, and I like it. I like you." I shrug a shoulder, feeling like a little bitch for putting it all out there. But isn't that what women want? Honesty?

I can see her fighting the small smile pulling at the corner of her lips. "I mean, what do you have lose, Kay?"

And look at me with my nickname for her already. If Philip was here, he'd take my man card and light in on fire.

"Everything." She sighs and retreats, pulling herself away from me.

"Seems like you already have." I realize what a dick I sound like when those words fall from my lips. "Let's see what you can find. There's a whole world out there—let me show it to you."

"This is crazy," she whispers and looks around her condo. "I can't just leave with you. I mean, I have to find a job. I need to figure out my life."

"There's no better time to take a little break, Kaylee. You have no responsibilities right now. There's nothing keeping you here. Come with me. Let the press settle down a bit here before you start looking for a new job. Plus, who's going to hire a teacher in the middle of the school year?"

"I hope someone will!" she shrieks. "I need money. I can't just gallivant around the world with you, Pax. I can't afford Europe."

"You're not paying for it, it's included in the film's press budget. It's two weeks, Kaylee. Just come with me. Give me two weeks."

She presses her fingers to her temples and rubs them in small circles.

"I promise you, it'll be worth it." I'm doing a lousy job of trying to convince her. I'm practically begging her. I'm about ready to revoke my own man card, *shit*.

She glances at me out of the corner of her eye. "Worth it for who?" she says, and I inwardly cringe at her remark.

"For both of us. Let's get to know each other better."

"Two weeks?" she asks and drops her hands to her side. I can see her brain ticking away inside her beautiful head.

"Just two weeks. Take this time to map out your next move." I take a few steps closer to her. "Take this time to get to know me better." I take a few more steps.

"What if I don't like you?" She smirks and props her hands on her hips.

"Then I'll send you home on a plane earlier." I loop my arms through the opening of hers and pull her to my chest. "But I promise, you're not going to want to go home early." I pull her into a hug.

"You're really cocky, aren't you?" she says against my chest.

"I like to call it confident. I'm really confident." I laugh at her.

"Call it what you want." She exhales in resignation, and I know I have her.

"How long do I have to pack?" She looks up at me.

I yank my phone from my pocket to check the time. "You have forty minutes."

She pulls herself from my embrace and begins frantically running up the stairs of her condo. "Make yourself comfortable," she hollers as she disappears up the stairs. I smile. If I could pat myself on the back, I would. Kaylee is coming to Europe with me.

My phone vibrates in my hand, and my euphoria is short lived when Kendall's name flashes across my screen.

"Kendall," I answer quietly and walk to the kitchen, as far away from the stairs as possible in hopes that Kaylee doesn't hear Kendall screaming through the phone.

"What in the ever-loving hell are you doing at that woman's house? Do you know it's on CNN right now? You are on goddamn CNN right now."

I sigh loudly into the phone. "I needed to make things right."

"That is not your goddamn job, that's mine," she screams at me. "Your job is to get your ass on that airplane in two-hours, your butt in the seat, and not talk to anyone. Do not talk to the press. Do not talk to your mother. Do not talk to ANYONE! Leave that goddamn house and that woman, get in your car, and get to the motherfucking airport. Do you understand me?"

"Ten-four." I end the call and smile to myself. That was one of Kendall's more epic meltdowns. I cannot wait to see what she says when she sees Kaylee's butt in the seat next to mine. I actually laugh out loud and brace myself all at the same time.

eleven

Kaylee

"One…two…three…go!"

Paxton gripped my hand even tighter as he darted out my front door. I clamored down the steps behind him, praying the lock on my townhouse actually caught because we weren't taking the time to make sure.

He made a beeline for a car parked across the lot. My huge suitcase he wheeled behind him with the opposite hand barely slowed us down.

I'm sure we made quite the sight.

What, with our heads down and our feet pounding across the pavement as if we were making a break for it.

We were.

And it was all caught on tape.

Of course, it was because the vultures had gone nowhere. They'd only gathered. As if they'd smelled blood and were circling overhead, just waiting for the right moment to dive in and take a good bite.

Oh wait, that was actually a helicopter.

Voices shouted, a slew of them vying to be the one to grab our attention. To get that one picture that would completely make their day.

As if this wasn't enough.

Lights flashed.

Click. Click. Click.

Paxton Myles!

Paxton!

Mr. Myles, can you confirm your relationship with Kaylee Rose Burton?

Kaylee…over here…is it true you're starring with Paxton in his next film that begins filming next month?

Were they serious right now? That alone was almost enough to make me stop and set things straight, but Paxton had given me strict instructions before we'd made our getaway.

Don't look up.

Don't answer.

RUN.

Paxton pressed a button on his key fob, and the trunk to a black car with even darker windows bounced open. He tossed in my suitcase and shut it just as fast. He moved even faster when he ran me around to the passenger side and hurried me in.

I'd barely blinked by the time he was sliding into the front seat and slamming shut his door. Frantic, he pressed a button to click the locks.

The sound of them engaging had us both breathing a sigh of relief, but adrenaline was still pounding through my veins.

Over the console, he looked across at me, his ridiculously handsome face cut in concern. Silence washed over us, his hands kneading on the leather of the steering wheel.

Our eyes met. Intense. Relieved. Searching for an answer for what in the hell we thought we were doing.

Then we both busted out laughing.

"Well, then," he said as he started the car, threw it in reverse, and backed out. He barely slowed as the paparazzi scattered, cameras pressing close to the windows to try to capture a blurry image.

"So, I'm totally getting the smoked-out windows now."

He chuckled, shifting into drive, the vantage definitely giving the scavengers the shot they were aiming for. "It's kind of a requirement for my line of work."

I seriously didn't know how any person could tolerate this kind of life. It was bad enough when I attended parties with Elle, the intrusiveness of the lenses. But even Elle was able to go back to her daily life without worrying someone was capturing something private.

I couldn't imagine dealing with this every single day.

Tires squealed when he hit the street, and he accelerated quickly, the whine of the engine loud as he gunned it, shifting gears faster than I could make sense of it

Clearly, he'd mastered the whole escape artist thing because he was weaving in and out of traffic, leaving no chance we'd been followed.

I sat back in the seat, finally allowing myself to take in my surroundings. My fingertips traced over the red stitching on the red and black leather, all the luxury and flash. "This car is ridiculous."

Those brown eyes brimmed with mischief when he glanced my way. "What...you don't like my Maserati? We can stop back at the house and grab a different car if it's not to your liking."

"Of course, we can," I mumbled under my breath.

He laughed. "You are a hard woman to please, Kaylee Rose. Here I was, being nothing but a considerate gentleman when I picked the one car in my garage I thought maybe was as pretty as you."

I swatted at his shoulder. "Oh, the charmer as always, Mr. Myles, rushing over to the castle of the damsel in distress to rescue her from certain demise."

A grin split his face. "At your service, ma'am."

I swatted him again. "You're not allowed to do that."

"Do what," he defended innocently, but there was absolutely nothing innocent about what was playing out in his eyes.

"Oh, don't *do what* me, mister. You know exactly what I'm talking about." I waved an overindulgent hand his way. "The accent...the face...the smile. Don't act like you don't use them to your benefit."

He shrugged, grinned as he changed lanes again and

accelerated as he took to the freeway. "What? A smart man uses any resources he has in his arsenal."

A pout pulled at my mouth. "Which is completely unfair if your opponent has absolutely nothing to stand up against them."

My mouth dropped open when he reached out and cupped my face. Tingles spread beneath his touch, and my stomach did about fifteen backflips. Of course, it had to settle right into the nausea from earlier, humiliation and defeat rising to the surface.

My voice dropped. "What are we doing, Paxton?"

I'd just been fired from my job that had been my entire life, had been hounded by paparazzi, and had been publicly shamed and ridiculed.

And now I was running off to Europe with the man who was the root of the problem.

A Greek god who owned the screen and commanded every audience. One who was sought after and adored.

My free card.

Funny, considering it'd cost me everything.

There wasn't anything *free* about it.

His thumb brushed softly under the hollow of my eye, catching the moisture I hadn't even realized had gathered there. "We're stealing you away from all of this."

I shook myself out of his hold and sat back in my seat. "That doesn't mean it's not all going to be waiting for me when I get back."

"You're right, Kaylee Rose. I'm not sure even I have the power to erase what happened this morning." The seriousness in his tone shifted, and a smirk went skating onto his mouth. "But I'm sure as hell going to make sure it's worth it."

Bewildered, I stumbled along beside Paxton as he strode through the international terminal at LAX. My suitcase had been checked and his apparently had been *handled*.

Must be nice.

Okay, I had to admit this *was* a little bit nice. I'd be nothing but a liar if I said it didn't feel *nice* with my hand firmly locked to his as we made our way down the long hall toward our gate.

"Right on time." He flashed me a grin.

"Doesn't the flight leave in like fifteen minutes?"

"Exactly. There's no use getting here and having to sit around for two hours. That's simply ridiculous."

"Says the guy who walks into a building packed with people and the waters part for him. I've never made it through security that fast...ever...even when I was returning after visiting my aunt in Kentucky and there was one person in front of me. And this is an international flight."

He lifted our entwined hands and brushed a soft kiss along the back of mine. A shiver tickled down my spine.

How did he manage that?

"Let's just call them the perks of being famous." He lifted a brow. Mischief danced in those warm brown eyes. "You witnessed some of the drawbacks back at your place today. What do you say we enjoy some of the advantages"

A short chuckle rolled up my throat. "That I did. I'm really not sure how you handle that part of this life."

He shrugged. "You get used to it. After a little while, it's little more than irritating."

In his pocket, his phone rang again, just like it'd been doing the last hour it'd taken us to get here. And just like then, he merely ignored it and let it go to voicemail.

One second later, it pinged with yet another new message.

"Are you sure you shouldn't answer that?"

This time both of his brows lifted, and his mouth quirked in a way that was so endearing I had the urge to pop up on my toes and press a kiss to his mouth. So I did.

A lick of fire.

His hand gripped the side of my waist, and he gave me a squeeze.

His phone pinged again.

"That is yet another drawback," he said with an exasperated sigh. That accent. It slipped out on the last, this time genuine. This time it wasn't used as a wicked tool to charm off my panties.

I figured the fact I was leaving the country with him pretty much guaranteed I was a sure thing.

God, I hoped so.

It rang again.

"It could be important," I countered.

He laughed. Almost both incredulous and affectionate. "Oh, I'm sure in her mind she thinks it's very important."

It was instant, the bolt of unease that shocked through me. She?

I wanted to ask. I had the right to, didn't I? But I really had no clue what this trip really meant or what I was getting myself into.

I hadn't even called my mother or my sisters. Even Elle didn't know where I was.

What was I doing?

Paxton suddenly pushed me backward, edging me back two steps and against the wall. My back pressed into it as he pressed into me.

Hard.

All of him.

He buried his nose in my hair and inhaled a deep, sharp breath. A sound of approval rumbled in his chest. I trembled as he ran the tip of his nose down the slope of my neck, shivered as he ran it back up. He left a slow, seductive kiss behind my ear.

The smolder turned molten. Hot and heated. An ache pulsed between my thighs.

His voice was a whisper, "Are you trying to freak out on me right now, Kaylee Rose?"

"I...I...uh..." I stuttered and stammered, trying to regain my senses as his tongue flicked out for a taste.

Oh. God.

That did not help.

"Do you think I can't see the panic written all over your face?" he murmured.

"I..."

"Are you thinking about bolting?"

"Um..."

I had completely lost the ability to form a coherent thought as he continued to lave kisses along my neck, as if we were on a secluded island rather than right out in the open at the airport.

People were probably taking pictures. Posting them to Instagram. Shaming me on Twitter.

#PaxtonMylesSlut

I didn't even care.

"I really hope you don't bolt on me, Kaylee Rose. Want to know why?"

"Mmmhmmmmmm." It was all an incoherent mumble beneath my breath.

What was that again?

"Because since the second I woke up and found my bed empty yesterday morning, all I've been thinking about is getting you back into it. Of ripping your clothes from this gorgeous body. Kissing you again. Tasting you again."

A whimper.

"Don't bolt, Kaylee…because when I get you to London, I'm going to fuck you. Hard then slow. Then I'm going to do it all over again. Don't make me chase you down this terminal and throw you over my shoulder, because I will. Or maybe I should take you into the executive club and give you a reminder of just what you'd be missing? How's that sound?"

Oh, yes and please.

"Final boarding call for flight 6816 with direct service to London Heathrow Airport…"

The overhead speaker broke into our little PDA sesh. The wall barely kept me from falling to my weakened knees when Paxton stepped back and gave me one of those earth-shattering smiles. The one that owned the screens and the hearts of the millions of fans who adored him.

I was certain right then it was going to be the one that crushed mine.

"Come on, before we miss our flight."

We scanned our boarding passes on our phones, and Paxton led me down the jetway. My heart beat erratically, with confusion and need and the internal whiplash this devastating man gave me.

A flight attendant greeted us at the door, and Paxton led me about four steps down the aisle to my seat.

First class.

Which was all kinds of ridiculous and luxurious and looked more like some kind of futuristic space pod than an airplane seat.

I settled down in the cozy space and stretched out my legs, accepted the flute of mimosa I was offered.

I allowed myself to sigh out a happy sigh.

After the insane day I'd had today, I was most definitely not going to complain.

"Is it to your liking, Ms. Burton?" he asked. Letting that southern charm come out to play, he exaggerated the words.

"Why yes, it is, kind, sir." A giggle escaped, and I was leaning forward to retrieve his kiss. We both froze when a low, enraged voice hit us like daggers.

"What the fuck is she doing here?"

Shocked, I looked up to find a woman glaring at me with the fire of a thousand suns. She was out of breath, as if she'd had to run to make the flight. A long, dark bob bounced around her shoulders when she turned the heat of her anger on Paxton.

He simply laughed and leaned back in his seat. "Nice to see you, too, Kendall."

"Are you fucking kidding me?" she hissed, leaning his direction so only he could hear. Oh, but I could. And maybe that's what she intended. "I've been calling you for the last two hours and Not. A. Word. I drove back to your house in case you'd fallen asleep. I almost missed this flight because you were off picking this up? I'd think *picking* her up once was enough, don't you?"

In horror, I looked over at Paxton for help. *Who is this woman?*

"Kaylee Rose, I'd like you to meet my favorite pain in the ass, the woman who thinks she's keeper of my life, my publicist, Kendall Stone. He glanced at her. "Kendall, meet Kaylee."

Kendall sneered at me without saying a word.

Great.

Yet another member of the #KayleeIsASlut fan club.

Apparently, I couldn't win.

Paxton was fast asleep. He'd had his seat turned into a bed, and for a few moments I allowed myself to just look at him. That beautiful face was almost as peaceful as it'd been when I'd snuck from his room two mornings ago.

Pushing out a breath, I got up and headed toward the small lavatory since I'd given up on getting any rest.

The lights had been dimmed for the redeye, and the narrow aisles were lit up in a path of lights to guide the way, like their own miniature runway. Only a few overhead lamps dotted the first-class cabin, most of the passengers making use of the time to sleep.

Locking the door behind me, I wet my face and gave myself a moment to clear my head.

To make sense of the opposing feelings that tumbled within me.

Excitement.

Heartbreak.

So contrary. But they were there.

Huffing out a cleansing breath, I unlatched the door and stepped out into the dimness of the aisle.

I gasped at the figure standing there waiting for me.

Dark, pin-straight hair. Hardened jaw. Flashing eyes. Arms crossed over her chest.

I guess this #KayleeIsASlut fangirl was stalking me now.

Awesome.

I touched my chest and forced a smile. "You scared me, Kendall."

Yeah, I called her by name even though I hadn't shared a word with her before. The only introduction I'd gotten from her was a livid sneer before she'd made her way to her seat three rows behind us.

Red lips stretched in a smile that was pure scorn. "Don't you dare stand there and give me the innocent act."

I gulped around the knot that formed in my throat. "I don't know what I did to you, but I can assure you—"

"What you did to me?" she interrupted. "Do you know what my job is, Kaylee Rose?" Her tone turned placating, as if I was dense and didn't have the capacity to understand.

I blinked. "You're Paxton's publicist."

"Right…that's my title. But do you know what I actually do? I'm the *trash* keeper. The one who comes in behind him to clean up all his messes. Do you have any idea how many people try to get close to him? Take advantage of who he is? All the sluts and gold diggers and aspiring actresses who will do absolutely anything to get close to him? It's my job to protect him from that. To keep him safe."

"I would never—"

"Do you know how many of Paxton's playthings I've dealt with? I let him have his fun, he gets his rocks off, and then I come in for the sweep. And let's just say that job keeps me plenty busy. Paxton knows the game. Hell, he hired me for it. But every once in a while…someone slips through the cracks…someone who looks so innocent and sweet, Paxton doesn't have the first clue what she's really up to."

Insecurity bubbled in my chest, and I fisted my hands. "I'm not trying to take advantage of Pax. I don't want anything from him."

She scoffed. "Then what are you doing here?"

"Spending time with him."

Low laughter rocked from her throat, and she edged forward. "Do you really think I'm that stupid? That clueless? Maybe Paxton is, but the truth of the matter is, he really doesn't have to worry about any of that, now does he? He doesn't have to deal with the consequences or the shit he leaves behind it. No. That's my job. And I'm damned good at it." She jabbed a red, manicured finger into my chest. "Don't think for a second that's going to change now."

She turned on her heel and moved down the lit pathway toward her seat. My hand shot out to keep myself from falling, and I forced myself to pull in deep breaths as I fought against the heartbreak that came rushing in to blot out the excitement.

What the hell was I doing?

Did I really think this was a good idea?

That this would solve any of my problems?

So I liked Paxton.

Actually *liked* him.

That definitely didn't change either of our circumstances.

Kendall's words spun through me. *Do you really think you're any different?*

Bitter laughter rushed up my throat. Maybe I had.

With my head held low, I shuffled back to my seat.

A small yelp left me when a hand snatched me around the wrist. Warmth spread, and I was hauled onto Paxton's lap. He was sitting up, my legs straddling his waist, my chest beating against his.

His insanely handsome face was barely visible in the shadows, his voice rippling with the accent that made my knees weak. "What the fuck did she say to you?"

"I don't… I don't want to cause any trouble for you Pax. I should just—"

"Fuck her." He cut me off. "Fuck her and whatever she told you or made you believe. Fuck her for making you question coming with me. I know she's looking out for me, because that's her job, but she doesn't always know what's best for me. She doesn't always know what *I want.*"

My head shook. "You don't even know me."

The reality was, I *could* be one of those girls. The premiere could have been a total set up. An elaborate plan Elle and I had concocted to get me *close* to the world's most sought-after bachelor.

But it wasn't. Our meeting hadn't been anything close to that.

Did that really matter to him or was this just another mess he was all too happy to leave Kendall to clean up?

He brushed the back of his fingers down my cheek, then cupped them in his big, strong hands. "No…you're right, Kaylee Rose. I don't. But I want to. These press junkets—the premieres and the parties—it gets so damned old, Kaylee. So old it blurs and becomes another part of the job. This is the first time I've been excited about one in years." He squeezed my face in emphasis. "Years. That's because of you. And I won't let her take that away."

"Pax."

His name came out so soft. In relief. In need. In all the confusion that had become my life.

He edged forward. His words were nothing more than a breath whispered near my mouth. "I could make a call and have just about any woman waiting in London for me, Kaylee Rose. But there's one I want. Only one I haven't been able to get off my mind."

He leaned in, his mouth murmuring against the sensitive flesh of my ear. "You."

I panted. Actually damned panted at a single word. Or maybe I was panting because of his body. Because of his possessive grip or his cock that grew hard and thick between us.

Oh, God.

I rocked against him, suddenly overcome with the need for this man to touch me.

"Kaylee," he murmured. His hands trailed down over my shoulders, tracing my ribs, before one hand was cupping my knee. He eased it up my thigh and under my skirt.

I inched up a fraction to make him room, and I bit down on my bottom lip when he dipped his fingers beneath my underwear and slicked his fingers through my folds. I buried a needy gasp in his neck when he brushed my clit.

He edged back to capture my attention. "I think you have the answer to every single one of those questions running through that pretty little head of yours *right here*, Kaylee Rose. Right here in this sweet pussy that is begging for more."

He pushed two fingers inside me, and my breath caught.

"Tell me you want more," he demanded.

"Yes."

I wanted more. I wanted everything.

He kept us nose to nose, his breaths clouding my senses as he lifted me higher and higher. My fingers dug into his shoulders as pleasure gathered fast, and part of me couldn't believe what I was doing.

On a plane.

But the part of me that'd agreed to follow him to London didn't care.

She was too caught up. Taken by this man in a way she shouldn't be.

And she was going to enjoy every second of it.

Pleasure rocketed through every inch of my body. I buried a scream in his shoulder when I came, riding wave after wave as he pressed a bunch of kisses to my forehead.

I shivered, and this gorgeous man smirked as he eased his fingers out of me, his sexy voice back to murmuring in my ear. "Let's go ahead and call that another one of the perks."

twelve
Paxton

With a small thud, our plane hits the ground in London. I can't take my eyes off Kaylee, but her eyes are glued to the new world outside the window of the plane. Her fingers grip the edge of her seat as her head bobs from side to side as we taxi to the gate.

When she finally pulls her attention back inside the plane, she turns to me with the biggest smile. Sheer excitement is written on her face, and she all but bounces excitedly in her seat.

"Ready?" I ask her as I unbuckle my seatbelt before the chime tells me I can. She nods quickly, unbuckling herself.

When the plane finally stops, I stand and stretch, catching sight of Kendall over my shoulder, her cell phone already pressed to her ear. She's sending me a non-verbal warning, a stern message with only her eyes as she has an entirely different conversation with whomever she's speaking with on the phone.

I gather Kaylee, pulling her in for a quick kiss as we deplane. With her tucked closely to my side, I don't bother to wait for Kendall. "Fair warning," I begin as we descend the jetway into the terminal. "The paparazzi are just as bad here as they are in L.A. They come out of nowhere and when you least expect it. Don't let your guard down, they're everywhere. Same rules apply. Don't say a word. Don't make eye contact. Just move."

"Got it." She pulls me tighter to her, her fingers pressing into my side. I hate that these vultures won't leave us alone, and instinctively I want to protect her from them. We're chauffeured into a line that's shorter and more obscure for our passport check—and I'm thankful for this. Kendall has caught up to us but keeps her distance—though I can feel her anger from ten feet away.

The passport check is quick, and we're on our way to claim our baggage in no time. Kaylee's fingers are laced through mine as we try to blend in with the crowds of other travelers. It's hard not to notice Kaylee's eyes darting from side to side, checking out every person in our path. Her fingers squeeze mine harder as the crowd lightens and we become more visible.

As we arrive at baggage claim, Kenneth, Kendall's 'right arm' in the UK, has all of our baggage already on a cart and is waving us in his direction.

"Paxton," he says in his thick British accent, offering me his hand to shake. "Good to see you, man." His handshake is firm and fast. Kenneth is the epitome of professional. He's direct, buttoned-up and doesn't play the bullshit games that Kendall does.

"And this must be the lovely Kaylee." He leans in and air kisses both of her cheeks. She blushes but offers him a courteous smile in return. "You two have really made a splash the last forty-eight hours," he laughs, holding onto her hand. "I'm Kenneth. Publicist extraordinaire on this side of the pond. But don't get too excited. You'll never be rid of her." He nods his head over Kaylee's shoulder just as we hear Kendall approach, her heels clicking on the tile floor.

He smirks at Kendall who ignores him and continues chatting away on her phone. "I see she's still charming as ever," he mumbles under his breath as he rolls his eyes.

"Now that you're all here, I have a car waiting. It's a shit show out there," he huffs as he pushes the luggage cart. "Head down. Walk fast. Don't take any questions."

"Pax already warned me," Kaylee politely tells Kenneth as we fall into line behind him.

"And here," he reaches for a pair of sunglasses he has tucked into his button up shirt. "Put these on. You look like shit." He shoves the sunglasses at me as Kaylee giggles.

I slide the Ray Ban aviator glasses on and pull Kaylee close to me as the large sliding glass doors open and the assault of flashing lights and questions begin.

"Paxton!"

"Pax!"

"Kaylee! We'd love an exclusive interview with you!"

The screams, questions, and flashes are overwhelming even for me, I can't imagine what Kaylee is feeling. She tucks her head into my chest, and I wrap a protective arm around her shoulders pulling her closer. Right where I want her, in my arms.

A large black SUV waits at the curb with the rear doors open. I begin walking us faster toward the car as Kenneth uses the luggage cart to his advantage, clearing a direct path to the waiting SUV. I damn near shove Kaylee into the back seat, before slamming the door behind us and locking it.

"Holy shit," she mumbles, brushing her hair out of her face. "Kenneth was right. They're just as bad here as back home."

"Fucking animals," I bark as the car is surrounded by flashing lights and people banging on the windows.

"Sir?" the driver says loudly, getting our attention. "Buckle up. We're going to be making a fast exit once we get our final passenger loaded."

Poor Kenneth is loading luggage into the back of the SUV as Kendall sits quietly in the front seat, face pressed to the window, ignoring Kaylee and I in the backseat. Kaylee shoots me a look of concern, and I brush it off with a shake of my head. Kendall can be a complete bitch when things don't go exactly her way. She's pouting, and I refuse to play her games.

With the slam of a door, Kenneth slides in next to Kaylee, sandwiching her between us.

"Go!" he hollers, and the driver makes the exit he warned us about, fast and abrupt. We're not even out of the airport when Kenneth pulls his phone out and begins dolling out orders.

"Pax," he begins. "Thursday night is the premiere. But

tomorrow you have an appearance on the Graham Norton show and interviews with the BBC and a whole shitload of radio interviews. Radio will be done from your suite bright and early. Kendall will take the lead on the radio. I'll be by with a car to take you to Graham Norton immediately following."

"Got it." I nod.

"That leaves some downtime for you and Ms. Kaylee to explore London. I can make arrangements for dinners or shows should you wish. Just ask, and I'll make it happen." I can't think of anything other than getting Kaylee naked and underneath me.

"Kaylee." He smiles at her and rests his phone on his leg. "A stylist has been busy shopping and has an entire rack of dresses for you to try on in the suite for the premiere. Hair and make-up will be there for you as well. Everything is taken care of."

Her eyes widen as Kenneth runs down the amenities that will be at her service. "Anything that's not there that you need, you ask me." He side-eyes Kendall to see if she has any reservations, but she still hasn't moved, her forehead still pressed to the window in the front seat.

"I can make almost anything happen, but time is of the essence. If you need something for tonight, you need to tell me soon." He looks at me when he says this. I'm sure he's thinking I'm going to ask him to get me at a table at an exclusive restaurant or one of the hot nightclubs. Fuck that. Tonight, it's all about me devouring Kaylee.

Kaylee takes a sharp breath and nods at him. "Thank you, Kenneth." She looks genuinely relieved that she doesn't have to worry about a damn thing.

"Pax." Kenneth turns his attention back to me. "For the interviews, both radio and television, I think it's best to stick strictly to questions regarding the movie. Everyone has been warned to avoid personal questions, but you and I both know those arse holes never stick to script. Avoid answering personal questions at all costs. Keep this about the movie. Kaylee's been through a lot—"

"Or just answer the fucking questions, Pax. It's what you'll do anyway. I'm not sure why you bother having publicists when you don't listen to a goddamn word we say," Kendall snaps from the front seat. Her voice is laced with venom and bitterness.

"There she is!" I blurt out, and Kaylee squeezes my hand, a silent warning to be kind. "Now that you're back with us, do you have any additional requests that Kenneth hasn't covered?"

She cocks her head and narrows her eyes, "Nope. It's all been covered."

"Excellent. Then let's all enjoy London." I sit back in my seat, and Kaylee visibly relaxes as the tension begins to ease in the car.

Our driver winds through the city before pulling up to The Ritz Carlton hotel where another crew of paparazzi are already camped out and waiting for us.

As we exit the vehicle, Kenneth pulls Kaylee aside to brief her on this whirlwind of a trip. I hear him telling her where she should stand during interviews, how to keep her focus and not let the flashes from cameras blind her, and most importantly how to smile at all times. Even when she's scared or worried...smile. I appreciate Kenneth providing her guidance as my mind is all over the place and Kaylee takes her crash course in publicity like a champ.

As I'm lost in my own thoughts, Kendall approaches, her lips pursed and fire in her eyes.

"There are no words to accurately describe how pissed off I am," she seethes, keeping her voice low so as Kaylee doesn't hear. "I'm doing everything in my power to keep—"

"Just stop, Kendall!" I muster, getting in her face. She takes a step backward to move away from me. It's rare I get aggressive with anyone, let alone Kendall, but she is fucking pissing me off. "Believe it or not, Kaylee is a good girl. She's here for the right reasons—"

"I don't care why she's here. I don't like it, and I want her gone."

"Kendall—" my voice warns. "Don't make me choose."

"Choose what?" she snaps.

"Between you and her...because you're not going to like who I pick." I raise my eyebrows in warning, and her eyes narrow into thin slits. "Kendall, please don't make this difficult for me. I like

Kaylee. A lot. I asked her to come with me. In fact, I begged her to come with me. She's different than the other girls."

Kendall snorts and rolls her eyes. "They're all *different*," she scoffs.

"Kaylee is different. I could see myself falling in love with this girl. She's *that* different."

Kendall's eyes widen at my admission, and she shakes her head. "And you know this after one night of being balls deep in her?" The sarcasm dripping from her voice continues to piss me off. "Just keep her close. I don't want to have to fucking deal with her," she says before turning on a heel and walking away.

I see Kaylee approach cautiously as we both watch Kendall walk away, with a frown on her face.

I put a big smile on my face and reach for Kaylee's hand. "Let's go get settled. I plan on taking advantage of our suite tonight." I press a kiss to the top of her head.

Turning to the bellman who has our baggage loaded on a luggage cart, I tell him, "Don't deliver those for a couple of hours. We won't be needing them right away." He nods at my orders, and I pull Kaylee towards the lobby of the hotel. I have one thing on my mind right now and it's devouring her for the next few hours.

thirteen

Kaylee

"Oh my God." I pressed my hand to my chest and spun in a circle as I took in my surroundings. "This can't be real. This is absolutely amazing. Gorgeous. I can't even. Paxton."

Awe dripped from every word.

We might as well have been staying at the Royal Palace for all the luxury of the over-the-top suite.

"Gorgeous," he said in a low voice. I turned that direction at the sound of his voice. Only he wasn't looking at the overindulgent luxury of the suite.

He was looking directly at me.

My breath caught when he began to stalk my direction.

The air grew thick and he slanted me one of those smiles that owned the world before he ripped his shirt over his head.

A stunned, "Oh," bled from my mouth.

Was that drool?

My gaze swept his body. With each step he took, his abs rippled and the muscles of his wide, strong shoulders flexed and bowed.

This…this was what fantasies were made of. It seemed impossible it could be my reality.

"Are we doing this…right now?" I asked as he began to back

me through the main room and into the bedroom waiting beyond.

"Oh, yes, Kaylee Rose, we are definitely doing this *right now.*" His voice dropped an octave. Slow and rough.

A tremor rolled down my spine, and my heart rate sped.

Desire twisted through my belly and pulsed between my thighs.

This felt so…different than the last time. Last time had felt like a secret. A memory to hold, never to be repeated again.

This felt like a statement.

Like a claim.

He took another step toward me. He pushed his fingers under my shirt and lifted it over my head. My hair tickled down around my shoulders, my breasts straining with need as cool air brushed my skin.

"Gorgeous," he whispered again. His fingertips trailed across the lace of my bra. The grin he wore grew wicked as he leaned around and flicked the snap and freed it. He slid it down my arms and took a step back to pull it free. "So damned gorgeous. Look at you. So pink and lush." His voice dipped in seduction. "The softest rose."

Chills skated, a rash of goosebumps lifting in their wake.

Paxton followed them with his fingers. "Do you feel that, Kaylee Rose?" He inflected the last as he edged me into the room that was just as extravagant as the first. I swore it was like stepping into a museum. "What I do to you?"

His slid his palms up my arms and over my shoulders. Purposefully, he ran them down my sides where his fingers dipped into the waist of my skirt. He tugged it free.

I yelped when he suddenly hauled me up and tossed me on the bed. A giggle filtered out, and I arched up on the bed as he tugged off my shoes.

He wound his fingers in the side of my underwear, hesitated for the briefest flash of a second, before he pressed a kiss between my thighs. "I like these."

He dragged them off.

"But I like you bare better."

Another giggle.

God. This so wasn't me. But it felt so good. Felt so right.

"I think I like you bare better, too."

"Is that so?"

Chewing at my bottom lip, I nodded, my hair billowing out across the pillow. "That's so."

A low chuckle rumbled in his strong chest. "I think that can be accommodated."

He flicked the button on his jeans and shrugged out of them.

My head spun.

One of the most sought-after bachelors in the world was standing in front of me. Hard. Ready. Wanting *me*.

All the reservations and questions I'd been feeling flew out the window.

I climbed to my knees and met him at the edge of the bed.

I pressed my mouth to the bristling muscle of his chest. "You're so beautiful. I can't believe I'm here…in this place…with you."

Hot hands scraped over my shoulders. "I don't want you anywhere else."

"I still don't get that, but I'll take it." It was almost a tease.

He laughed, the sound a lure. "Oh, you're going to take it, all right."

Shivers danced, and I started kissing down his chest, over the hard, hard planes of his six-pack that flexed and bunched beneath my lips. My tongue licked out for a taste.

All man.

He wrapped his hands in my hair, fisting it tight when I got to the band of his underwear.

I peeked up at him as I slowly lowered them.

He shrugged out of them and increased his hold.

"Take me into your mouth."

Lust rocked me to the core. I liked it. Liked that he wasn't afraid to demand what he wanted. Liked it more when he groaned when I pressed my lips to the tip. My tongue explored, before I took him deeper.

His stomach jerked and ticked, and he left one hand tangled in my hair while the other came to the side of my face as he began to guide me up and down his length. His hips rocked in time.

Needier. Deeper. Harder.

"Fuck," he cursed. He pulled free. A shocked gasp left me when he suddenly pulled me up from my knees. The man devoured my mouth, tongue and teeth and lips, before he was pushing me back into the middle of the bed.

"I need to get inside of you, Kaylee Rose. Right now."

Almost frantic, he dug around in the basket filled with necessities that had been left bedside.

My mouth watered as I watched him roll a condom over his cock.

He climbed onto the bed and wedged himself between my knees.

He leaned down close to my ear. "Hold on."

I did exactly what he said, my fingertips digging into the skin of his shoulders as he tucked my knee over his hip.

He filled me in one solid thrust.

"Paxton." It was a throaty moan.

"Fuck…so good. I fucking love the way you feel. So damned perfect," he mumbled as he pulled out then rocked back in, stealing my breath. He was quick to pick up a rigid pace. Hard and long. Deep and demanding. So, so good.

He pushed up to his hands, looking down at me as he took me whole.

I forgot who I was.

Where I was.

The only thing I was in that moment was his.

"Touch yourself," he commanded, and my hand fluttered down my belly.

He groaned when I brushed my fingers into my folds, my first two fingertips running circles around my clit.

"So hot. Shit…you're so hot. Look at you. Look at you."

We both watched down where we were joined. His hips snapped and my fingers strummed my body.

Pleasure wound fast. So thick I swore I could see it hovering in the air.

Every muscle on his gorgeous body tightened, and I rocked up, desperate to meet him thrust for thrust.

I'd never felt anything like this.

Not once in my life.

Not ever.

He sat back on his knees and wound his arms under my hips, lifting them from the bed. The magnitude of the shift hit me from every side, consumed with the way his body filled mine.

So full.

So much.

So good.

Bliss broke. It sped through my nerves, saturating every cell.

I cried out, and he increased his pace, harder and faster as he pulled every ounce of pleasure from my body. He shouted my name, his hips erratic before he stilled, his hands gripping me tight.

I could feel the intensity of his orgasm, as fierce as mine.

Mind-bending.

Heart-stopping.

I couldn't breathe.

He laughed when he toppled down at my side. "That was…"

"Incredible," I said.

"Amazing," he returned.

"Mind-blowing."

"Unforgettable." It was the truth. It didn't matter where we ended up. I was never going to forget this.

His smile softened as he ran his fingers through my hair. "Thank you for coming with me. You don't know what it means to me."

"I wouldn't want to be any other place."

His brow arched. "Really?"

I searched within myself for the truth. "Really."

He grinned. "That's good, because I wouldn't let you leave."

I could feel the heat flame to my cheeks.

"Come on, get up. I need to feed you."

"Do I have to?" It was only half a tease.

He smacked my ass, and I yelped. "Yes, you have to. You're going to need your energy for everything I have planned for you. Now get that fine ass out of my bed."

"Bossy," I told him as I gathered the sheet and wrapped it

around my body.

A smirk lifted one side of his mouth. "You have no idea."

fourteen

Paxton

"Mmmm..." Kaylee mumbles, her eyes still closed, as I run a finger over her shoulder and down her arm. After spending all of yesterday doing radio and television interviews, we spent most of last night in bed after a quick dinner at one of London's newest and most posh restaurants, and I know she's tired, but I have a full day planned for her.

"Mornin', sweet Kay." I brush my nose over her cheek before pressing my lips to her.

"Morning," she moans as she stretches her lean body out underneath the silk sheets. I toss my arm across her bare stomach and pull her over, cradling her in my arms. She slides a leg between mine and brushes her hand over my hardening cock, stopping to cop a feel.

I stop her, capturing her hand in mine before flipping her gently onto her back and settling between her legs. Heaven. She pants and writhes underneath me as I align myself at her entrance, teasing her. "As much as I want to stay in bed all day and devour you, I have something fun planned for us today." I rub my cock up and down her wet folds.

"Pax," she growls as I slide into her. I take it slow with Kaylee this morning, exploring every inch of her beautiful body as I make love to her. I make a note to touch every crevice, every soft, supple inch of her skin as we connect. Never have I wanted to take my time like this before, memorizing every single curve of this beautiful woman's body.

Most women satisfied an immediate need for me. A quick roll in the sheets, a means to an end. I got off, they left. End of the story. With Kaylee it's different. I never want it to end. I can't get enough of her. What the hell is she doing to me?

As we climax together, I can feel our hearts beat wildly against each other's chests.

"Kay," I mumble against her neck as my lips pull gently at her soft flesh as I try to catch my breath.

"Hmm," she answers in response, her own breathing labored.

"Thank you for coming to London with me."

She doesn't answer, but I can feel her smile against my shoulder as we both come down from our climaxes. I know she's nervous as hell about being here with me, about us, but I can't imagine being anywhere without her.

"Where are we going?" Kaylee smiles as I pull her quickly through the hotel lobby, hoping we go unnoticed. Kenneth sent a car and security detail for us, along with an agenda outlining everything we'll be doing for the next eight hours. I plan to show Kaylee everything London has to offer.

"You'll see when we get there," I pull her in tightly next to me, wrapping an arm around her shoulder. I nod at the driver waiting in the carport with the backdoor of the large suburban open and waiting for us to slide into.

Once inside, we meet the two burly men who will tag along with us today.

"Paxton."

I reach out and shake each man's hand.

"William." The first man introduces himself with a firm handshake.

"Michael." The second does the same.

As he pulls from the curb, Michael goes over their plan for keeping us safe, but not smothering us, and I'm so appreciative that Kenneth thought to get us security. I want to spend my day focusing on Kaylee, not worrying about any shenanigans happening around us.

"No autographs today. No selfies. No fan pictures," I tell them. "I just want to spend the day with Kaylee and feel normal for once."

Kaylee squeezes my hand, and I take a deep breath. Each man nods in understanding, and I feel comfortable that they know how to handle all the "celebrity baggage" that always accompanies me.

"Pax," Kaylee gasps, her face pressed up against the tinted window. "It's a Ferris wheel!"

"Oh, sweetheart, it's more than a Ferris wheel. Just wait." The driver pulls up and parks as William and Michael exit first. We follow suit just as another man rushes over. Neither William or Michael blink at the man who extends his hand in greeting to me.

"Paxton Myles, I'm Rob Doherty, your tour guide for today." Right, tour guide. I remember seeing something in Kenneth's message that we'd have a tour guide. "We'll be starting here at the London Eye, and I have a couple of other amazing things to show you." He extends his arm toward the giant wheel, guiding us toward the entrance.

As we approach the area to board, Rob continues, "The Eye is all yours for the next hour. No one will be in your capsule, or any other capsule. The most magnificent views of London you'll ever see. Be sure to look for The Houses of Parliament, Big Ben, Westminster Abbey, Buckingham Palace, The Tower Bridge, and of course the River Thames." His smile is huge and infectious and Kaylee's matches.

He steps inside the capsule to point out a table that has been set up with champagne and orange juice. "Enjoy champagne or mimosas while you're up there, but mostly enjoy the view. It's spectacular!" He steps out of the capsule while they close the door and Kaylee stands speechless.

"You okay?" I give her hand a gentle squeeze. "Please tell me you're not afraid of heights." I chuckle, but panic for a quick moment, having not even considered asking her prior to booking this. She looks up at me, her eyes wide, her face somber.

"Paxton Myles, I can't even believe you've gone through the trouble of doing this for me. It's too much, it's too…" She pauses, blinking as she takes in the surroundings. Clearing her throat, she looks back up at me. "It's too amazing." She takes a deep breath as the capsule jolts slightly as we begin to rise. "And no, I'm not afraid of heights."

I pull her into my arms, and she wraps hers around my waist in return. I could get used to this. Her next to me…all the time. Her cheek pressed to my chest as the capsule rises slowly and we take in all of London's beauty.

It takes about an hour to make two full rotations. I made sure to point out all of the landmarks that Rob mentioned for us to look for, and Kaylee was fascinated. Her eyes beamed in awe, and it was so fucking cute when she'd laid eyes on all these pieces of London's history while sipping on champagne.

As we disembark the London Eye, Rob, William, and Michael wait for us and lead us back to the Suburban.

"Was it everything you'd hoped it would be?" Rob asks Kaylee.

"More." She looks up at me. That's exactly how I felt as well. While seeing London is amazing, it's Kaylee that makes it better.

"I agree," I say quietly, lacing her fingers through mine.

Once we're settled back in the car, Rob pulls out his phone and smiles. "Next up, private tour of Buckingham Palace."

Kaylee's eyes about bug out of her head. "What does that mean?" she asks, softly.

"It means Rob here is giving us a private tour of the Palace." I nudge her with my shoulder and press a tender kiss to her temple. Her excitement brings me happiness. Is this what it feels like to be in love? When your happiness takes a back seat to someone else's? I tuck away that thought and smile at Kaylee.

"We'll get to see the State rooms, the Queen's Gallery, and the Royal Mews. We won't be with anyone else, so we can take our time and we get access to additional areas the general public doesn't get to see." Kaylee shakes her head in disbelief.

"Come here," she whispers, pulling me toward her, pressing her forehead to mine. "You are too much, Pax, but thank you. Thank you so much." She kisses me, deeply. A kiss that feels so much more than all the others. This kiss bears the weight of what she's feeling, and fuck if it doesn't about make my heart explode.

"Unbelievable," is all she can say when we exit Buckingham Palace. She's been quiet for the last hour, I expect she's about as overwhelmed as I am having taken in all the history and splendor of the Palace.

"It really was, wasn't it?" I stop and look around. We've gone unnoticed, mostly thanks to the private tour and shutting down the London Eye for an hour. It feels good to feel like every other normal person who's out and about sightseeing.

"What's wrong?" Kaylee asks as I eye St. James Park off in the distance.

"Nothing. Michael, William," I nod my head toward the park and both men give me a look. "Just a little detour, Kay." I press a kiss to the top of her head. "Come on."

The two men fall into step behind us as I guide her toward the beautiful park. While it's overcast today, I put my sunglasses on in hopes it hides my face and we can continue to go unnoticed. William and Michael stay a bit closer to us here in the open public, but people don't seem to notice me, thank God. At the entrance of the park, we stop to look at the beautiful flower beds which are bright and colorful. Kaylee snaps a quick picture of them with her phone before we continue on.

"Pax," Kaylee sighs as she lifts her phone and snaps another picture of the fountain in the middle of the lake.

"Yes, Kay?"

She shoves her phone into the back pocket of her jeans and looks up at me. "This might be the best day I've ever had. Thank you."

I smile back at her. "You've thanked me no less than fifty times today." I rub my thumb over her bottom lip, wanting to suck the soft flesh between my teeth.

"No one has ever done something this nice for me before."

"I want to do nice things for you all the time, Kaylee. So, get used to this, and stop thanking me." I pull her in for a hug.

"Mr. Myles," William says, interrupting our moment. "We best get going." He nods his head toward a crowd of people who are all holding up their cell phones snapping pictures of my moment with Kaylee.

"Fuck," I hiss under my breath. "Ready, baby?" Kaylee nods, sliding her hand into mine as Michael and William get us back to the car safely.

fifteen
Kaylee

Paxton held open the door to the massive suite. "Ladies, first," he said, shooting me one of those earth-shattering grins, all white teeth and Southern charm as he bowed down and gestured for me to go ahead of him.

A giggle slipped free. After the day we'd shared, I couldn't help it. The outright giddiness that swept through me. "Why, thank you, kind sir." My words oozed playfulness as I dipped down into an exaggerated curtsy.

Fingertips fluttered out to graze down the side of my neck, his words lifting chills where he whispered them at my ear, something about them both possessive and sincere. "I'd do anything for my lady."

My heart rate spiked as my mind struggled to catch up with what was happening between us.

Today had been one of the best days of my life, seeing all the history of London, things I'd never gotten to experience before and probably never would have had Paxton not invited me along.

Under any circumstances, it would have been wonderful. A once in a lifetime chance.

But it was Paxton who'd made it magical.

This morning while riding The London Eye, I'd seen some of

the most notable landmarks in all the world.

But I knew, when I thought back to tonight, to this trip, it would be Paxton's face that I remembered.

The realization of that sent a tumble of apprehension through me, knowing this was going to hurt when it all came to an end. Because I liked Paxton Myles more than I should probably admit. In a way that had become so much more than one night.

Trying not to think about the future, I forced myself to smile at him from over my shoulder. "I'm going to go freshen up."

Hands stuffed into his pockets, he rocked back on his heels and cast me the sweetest smile. "Don't be long. I'll miss you."

"Sure you will." It was the barest tease and I knew I needed to get out of there with the way the man was looking at me. With the way he just kept getting deeper and deeper under my skin.

I headed into the bedroom and into en suite restroom, toed off my shoes, and let my hair down.

I tugged my shirt over my head, then gasped a little breath when I looked up into the mirror to find Pax standing right behind me.

"Pax."

Really, I shouldn't have been all that surprised. But I guess what had caught me off guard was the look in his eye right then.

I thought maybe it was different than anything that had ever been there before.

Intense and determined.

He edged forward and my heart hammered.

His gaze never wavered from mine as he looked at me through the mirror as he reached up and unwound the shirt I had clutched in my hand.

"Let me help you with that," he murmured, his breath skating the bare flesh at the crook of my neck.

Chills rushed down my spine.

He inched even closer, his chest grazing my back as he let his palms slide down the outside of my arms as he leaned in and whispered at my ear, "I saw what just flashed through your eyes, you know." His words sounded like a quiet demand. "I saw exactly what you were thinking."

"And what was that?" I barely managed around the thick knot that rose in my throat. A knot lifted by the sudden intensity that had gathered in the tiny space.

So fierce I was sure the man's presence had become an entity of its own.

His hands skated back up my arms, running over the caps of my shoulders before he was winding my hair in one hand, angling my head to the side as he pressed his mouth to my pulse that was thrumming wildly in my throat. "You were thinking about the end, Kaylee Rose. You were thinking about the night when I don't get to make love to you before we fall asleep and the morning I don't wake up with you in my arms."

"I'd be a fool if I didn't think that day wasn't coming."

Then why did the thought of that rip me apart inside?

God, I'd let myself get so damned deep, coming here with him, getting swept up by the whirlwind that was Paxton Myles.

Being with him made me feel as if I was the only woman in the world. As if when he looked at me, I had become his focal point.

I shrugged a shoulder, though it took about all the energy I had to do it. "We don't even know each other, Pax. Today was…"

Wonderful.

Amazing.

I want to do it over and over and over.

Never let it go.

Never let you go.

"…Unforgettable. But you and I? We're from very different worlds."

He gave my hair a little tug. "Who says those worlds can't become one, Kaylee Rose? Who says?"

An incredulous chuckle escaped my lips. "I'm pretty sure about every person in the whole damned world."

"And I say fuck the whole world because I want you to be a part of mine."

I blinked at him through the mirror. "We barely know each other."

He released my hair and set both his hands on my waist. He pressed himself against my bottom. "And that doesn't change the way we feel, does it? These last few days…"

He paused, his tongue darting out to wet his lips, as if he were gathering himself, trying to find the right words. "The last few days have been the best of my life, Kaylee. The best. I invited you to come with me because I couldn't stop thinking about you. Because for the first time in years, I was actually excited about something. About *someone*. And I don't want that to end."

"What are you saying?" I asked him, the words breathless.

He cocked one of those grins. The kind that captivated the world on the screen. And tonight …it was fully directed at me. "I'm saying I want us to figure this out, Kaylee Rose. That when I step out, the whole goddamned world knows that I'm taken. That I belong to you and you belong to me. That you're mine. No speculation or questions. We just are."

Flooded with emotion, a tear slipped free. "You want me?"

He groaned and pressed himself closer to my back, and he buried his mouth in my hair as he muttered the words at the top of my head. "God, yes, Kaylee. I want you. That's obvious enough, isn't it? I want all of you. What do you say? Do you want all of me, too?"

He was back to flashing me that grin through the mirror.

So confident and sweet.

"As if you don't already know the answer to that," I said, swatting at the tear staining my cheek.

"You're willing to try this out with me?" he prodded.

I spun around to face him. "God, Pax, of course I am. How could I not? You are so different than I ever could have imagined. I've never felt like this."

He hugged me against him and pressed a kiss to my temple. "Good. Now that that's settled, get your fine ass in that bed."

Leaning back, I grinned up at him. "Always ordering me into your bed, huh?"

A chuckle rippled from his strong chest. "I think you'd best get used to it, Kay. You're going to be spending a lot of time in it."

"Is that a threat or a promise?" I let the tease wind into the words, my happiness too big to contain.

Because Paxton Myles had just become mine.

He stepped back and jerked his shirt over his head, one side of his mouth quirking up in a delicious grin, mischief playing in his eyes. "Both."

sixteen

Paxton

"Red or black?" Kaylee dangles a hanger holding two very different dresses from each of her forefingers. Except I'm not looking at the dresses. I'm looking at Kaylee standing stark naked, her perfect body on full display. Her breasts heavy and nipples taut. The curve of her hip teasing me as she waits for my answer. Snapping out of it, I answer.

"When in doubt always wear red," I respond, stepping into the shower.

She gives each dress another look and hangs the black one back on the garment rack. As I shampoo my hair, I watch her through the glass-encased shower. She twists her hair up on top of her head and collects an armful of bottles before opening the shower door.

"Hope you don't mind company," she says, her eyes dropping to my growing erection. All she has to do is be within a foot of me and I can't control myself. Her voice cracks as she watches me lather body wash on my chest. "The hair and makeup people will be here in twenty minutes and I need to rinse off."

I lick my lips as goose bumps pepper her skin and her nipples form into hardened peaks. "I only need ten minutes to do what I plan to do with you," I growl at her.

ONE **WILD** NIGHT

I reach for her arm, pulling her to me. My dick is growing harder when I see how affected she is by me. Water runs in a stream over her shoulders, through the valley of her breasts, and down the apex of her thighs to the spot I want to devour over and over again.

I move her behind me, turning to press her back against the marble wall, and she gasps when her back makes contact with the cool stone. Her eyes are heavy as she watches me position her exactly how I need her, sliding a knee between her legs. She widens her stance just slightly to make room for my leg.

I drag my tongue across her collarbone, nibbling at the soft flesh as my fingers pinch a hardened nipple causing her to elicit a deep moan. "Put your hands on my shoulders," I mumble against her neck.

Her trembling hands land on my shoulders as my palms trace the curves of her body resting on her perfectly round ass. Her eyes find mine, just as I lift her and she gasps loudly.

Our chests are pressed together, allowing me to feel the rapid beat of her heart. Her knees are spread wide, allowing me access to the very part of her I need right now. My dick presses against her warm center, and I look to her for permission.

Her head falls back as I press against her, still waiting for her to allow me into her.

"Kaylee," I growl against her neck as she rocks her center gently across my thigh. Her arms tighten around my neck as she lifts herself away from me. Disappointment floods through me, but then she suddenly lowers herself right on top of me, and now it's me that's groaning.

"Jesus Christ, Kay," I hiss as I fill her completely. She's seated on me all the way to the root, her tight walls expanding to take me in. "I'm not going to last long, you feel so fucking good." I begin to thrust, fast and needy. I'm overwhelmed by Kaylee and how fucking amazing she feels.

"You said you only needed ten minutes," she teases me.

I won't last ten goddamn minutes if she continues like this. She rocks her hips harder against me, fucking me as I hold her pressed against the shower wall. Her hands find my face, and she tilts my head up so she can kiss me. Our tongues dance with each other as she rocks her hips back and forth, fucking me. She twists her fingers in the hair at the nape of my neck as her orgasm builds. I can feel her fighting against it, but little does she know I'm ready to come along with her.

"Pax," she pants my name over and over again as I take over and slam into her. "I'm so close." Her eyes close and her head falls back against the marble as I continue to fill her, harder, and deeper than I've ever been before. Everything about her in this moment is beautiful. Her vulnerabilities. Her trust. Everything.

"Just feel it, Kaylee," I say as I thrust into her one last time, filling her to the hilt. She wraps her arms around my neck tighter as her entire body comes undone. Her thighs shake around me, and her entire body writhes between me and the wall, and I finally lose it along with her, filling her with my release.

I slide out of her, gently setting her to her feet. She steadies her wobbly legs and finally looks up at me with wide, innocent eyes.

"What are you doing to me?" I whisper.

She chews on her lip and her lips twist into a perfect smile. "The same thing you're doing to me." And that is when I fall head over heels for Kaylee Rose Burton.

"Don't be nervous," I whisper in Kaylee's ear as her death grip on my hand tightens even more as our limo approaches the theater. She has barely said two words since we left the hotel, but I can't keep my eyes off her. Her hair is styled up with a few locks of soft curls bouncing around her shoulders. She looks stunning in the fitted red dress that displays every fucking perfect curve of her body.

"Don't be nervous," she mocks me. "I want to hurl right this second and we're not even out of the car yet."

As we roll to a stop, the back door of the limousine opens quickly. I glance to my left and give her hand a little squeeze. "This is easy. Just smile. Don't answer any questions. Remember everything Kenneth told you." She inhales sharply and offers me a tight smile. She's so out of her element, but goddamn it, this is exactly where she's supposed to be.

With me.

I offer her an encouraging smile in return. "Ready?"

Wit is her trademark, and I'd expect nothing less from her in this moment. "As I'll ever be."

"Then let's do this." I slide out of the back seat carefully, never dropping her hand. The moment my feet hit the ground, the yelling, screaming, and flashes of light begin. I raise my right hand to offer the press a short wave as I help Kaylee exit the car as gracefully as possible in a floor length fitted gown.

She pulls herself tightly to my side as she puts a giant smile on her face. She's made for this. Her red lips are pulled to perfection as her eyes twinkle in the light bulb flashes.

"Kaylee!" The yells begin for her now. Security ushers us slowly down the red carpet to the step and repeat backdrop where we'll stand for pictures.

"Keep smiling, Kaylee. This is where I want you to focus on one thing and don't take your eyes off it. The lights will blind you if you try to look at the cameras."

We step up to the wall, standing in front of a giant image of my face from the movie poster. Kenneth stands off to the side, waiting to take us to the press line.

He arrived in a separate car just ahead of us. A clipboard pressed tightly to his chest, he smiles proudly as Kaylee does exactly as she's been told. Kenneth works the press line like a pro, getting me in and out in less than ten minutes.

"That wasn't so bad, was it?" I growl in Kaylee's ear as we're ushered to our seats in the theater.

With a small laugh, her lips pull upward. "Maybe for you. For me it was pure torture."

"Get used to it. This is the first of many," I respond, reassuring Kaylee that this is exactly where I want her. By my side. Tonight. Tomorrow. *Forever?* I shake the thought from my head and turn my attention to the screen just as the lights begin to fall.

The applause is startling…humbling actually. Cheers, whistles, and hoots fill the theater as the credits roll. My heart pounds and my cheeks flush at the standing ovation. Kaylee leans in and presses a sweet, long kiss to my lips. "Simply amazing," she says, her soft lips brushing mine as she speaks.

"You think so?" I ask, and she nods her head swiftly.

"Except for that part where you were naked in bed with that—"

My laugh cuts her off. "I like it when you're jealous. It's cute."

"Not jealous, just—" She pauses, thinking about how she's going to position this.

I answer for her. "Jealous. And I love it." I've been throwing that love word around a lot today, and it's totally unlike me. She rolls her eyes and smirks. Kenneth weaves through the crowd, his head bobbing up and down through the mass of people. When he finally reaches us, he wraps his hand around Kaylee's arm, tugging her gently toward him.

"I'm going to take you with me to the green room. Everyone wants to congratulate Pax, and it's *safer* there."

I know exactly what he means by safer. Safer from the press. Safer from Kendall, who's lurking nearby, and safer from the overwhelming atmosphere that movie premiere's entail. Kenneth senses Kaylee's unease, and honestly, the faster I can bullshit with these people, the sooner we can be out of here. The people can be stifling. I appreciate Kenneth looking out for Kaylee, and I shoot him an appreciative glance.

I pull Kaylee to me, wrapping my arms around her waist. Her entire body hums at my touch. I can't wait to be buried inside her again in a couple of hours. I grow hard thinking about the way her entire body quivers when she comes, or how her back arches when I slide into her.

I drop my forehead to hers, and she closes her eyes. "Go with Kenneth. I won't be long." She sighs and kisses the side of my mouth. "And in no more than two hours, I want those lips wrapped around my cock again."

"Pax," she hisses and slaps my chest jokingly.

"I'm serious. I want all of you, Kaylee." Her lips, her body, her heart. What the fuck has happened to me?

"Then all of me you'll have." She pulls back, her eyes finding mine. She could tell a million stories with those eyes. I see her fear, but also her sincerity. She's like no one else I've ever met. Kenneth reaches for her arm, pulling us out of our moment.

"I'll take good care of her. Now go mingle." He pats her arm and waves me off. I watch him guide her toward the side exit of the theater, and I'm anxious to get this over with so I can get back to my girl.

seventeen
Kaylee

"I hope you'll be comfortable in here. Paxton shouldn't be too awfully long." Kenneth hovered at the green room door, as if he were torn between staying there to watch over me and stepping back out with Paxton where he really belonged.

I threaded my fingers together. "I'll be fine, thank you."

He gestured with his chin toward the elaborate wooden buffet that was set up against the far wall. "Help yourself to whatever you need. And if you need anything else, call."

Warmth spread through my chest, and I nodded back as a small smile touched the corner of my mouth. "Thank you for watching out for me. I truly appreciate it."

With a curt nod, he exited the room and let the door fall shut behind him. It muted the bustle of voices and laughter that filtered in through the main room. Voices and laughter that vied for the attention of the man who had somehow managed to steal all of mine.

All of my focus.

All of my sanity.

Honestly, I was grateful to step away so I could get a breath. Grateful to have the time to process what I'd just experienced. Watching the movie at Paxton's side had been a jarring, stark reminder of who this man was. A reminder of his talent and fame. A reminder of the demands of his life and the brilliance he brought to the screen.

I was still having a hard time processing that I was here at the premiere in London.

At his side.

By tomorrow morning, I would be plastered all over the tabloids again. This time by choice.

I kept scrambling around inside myself, searching for reservations. I kept waiting for reason and logic to finally set in and remind me of who I was and who I'd always wanted to be.

I was a kindergarten teacher.

A girl who'd always wanted a modest and simple life.

A roar of laughter echoed from the walls.

And this?

This didn't even come close to a semblance of simple.

God…I couldn't even bring myself to call it *normal.*

It was a fantasy.

Impossible.

And here it was…right in front of me.

Moving toward the sidebar to pour a drink, I dropped my head and fought an affected smile when I was struck with the realization.

This was exactly where I wanted to be.

Here.

With him.

Despite the cameras and intrusion. Regardless of the gossip and the speculation.

I didn't care.

I reached for the bottle of champagne that was chilling in a silver bucket on the table, then stilled when I felt the air rustle from behind.

A cold, unwelcome chill.

It slithered across my skin like an omen.

I allowed myself to close my eyes for one second, before I gathered all the courage and resolve I had and slowly turned around to face the fierce presence that had appeared at the door.

"Kendall." It was barely a whisper.

She smiled a vicious, red-lipped smile, her bob brushing her thin, bare shoulders, the woman a knockout in her cobalt blue strapless dress.

If I didn't know better, I would have guessed her to have been one of the stars on the screen.

"I do hope you enjoyed the show." Her voice was all feigned interest and concern. "Although, I suppose you already slithered your way in to see it once. It doesn't have quite the same impact the second time around, does it?"

I stood my ground, refusing to let this woman belittle me just by her condescending tone.

"Actually, I think I appreciated it more the second time around...anticipating what was next. Knowing it would steal my breath and then being floored by it all over again."

She laughed. "Kudos to you, Kaylee. You do always seem to know the right thing to say." She wandered deeper into the room. "Though that doesn't change the situation, does it?"

Unease fluttered through my senses.

The last thing I wanted was another confrontation with this woman.

I respected her simply for the fact Paxton employed her, and he trusted her to look out for his best interest.

But she needed to understand I was there because of Paxton.

Because he wanted me there and I wanted to be there with him.

Because I cared about him and he cared about me.

My chin lifted a fraction. "I don't know what situation you're talking about."

She scoffed. "There's no need to play coy, Kaylee. You've known what this was right from the very start. You served your purpose and Paxton served his."

My head shook, and I took a step back as she came closer. "What are you talking about?"

Her voice dropped into something wicked. "You think you're really different, don't you? Did you actually come here thinking you were going to make *the Paxton Myles* fall for you? Did you really think you were going to manage to sink your claws into him so deeply they would actually stick?"

She edged in closer, so close to my face I could almost taste the venom when a condescending tsk jetted from between her lips. "You don't mean anything. You aren't any different than any of the thousands of other girls he's taken to his bed. He used you...fucked you...took you...and you let him. But don't worry, he's more than willing to compensate you for your time and effort."

Dread pushed at my chest. Heavy and dense. I took another floundering step backward, desperate to put space between us. "You're wrong. Paxton...he...he cares about me."

I needed to get out of there. I kept moving back. Needing air so I could think.

She took another step toward me. When she did, my back hit the wall.

She pulled an envelope from her black velvet clutch. "Paxton wanted me to make sure you had this."

Tears pricked at my eyes. "You're lying."

She tore the small slip of paper free from the envelope.

A check.

A check for *One-hundred Thousand Dollars*.

Nausea spun, and I choked back a sob. "No...Pax...he wouldn't..." The refusal stammered from my tongue.

Images flashed.

Ones of us from earlier in the hotel room.

The shower.

More slammed me. Picture after picture of the gorgeous women who'd been on his arm—gone the next day.

"No." It was a whimper.

Her head angled to the side. "Then why do you think you're in here and Paxton is out there? Why do you think he removed you from his side and left you in this room all by yourself? He's had his fun and now he's bored with you, Kaylee. Now it's time for you to go home."

I fought it. God, I fought it, but a single tear slipped free. I gritted my teeth against it, just as hard as I tightened my hands into fists. "No."

She lifted the check. "He signed it, Kaylee. This is his goodbye. Now…we have a driver waiting for you out back to take you to pick up your things at the hotel. You need to be at the airport in ninety minutes to catch your flight."

Anger burned.

So hot.

So unlike me.

But it was there, this ripping ache that felt too much like heartbreak.

She shoved the check at my chest.

I tore it out of her hand.

She stepped back, her grin nothing but a cruel *I told you so.*

I gripped it in a ball. "You think I want this?"

"Isn't that what everyone wants? Money? Fame? The chance to step out of their pathetic lives just for a second, to glean a taste of what it might feel like to live on the other side? You got your fifteen seconds, Kaylee. It's over. And I promise you, if I ever see you anywhere next Paxton Myles again, I will personally see to it that you regret it for the rest of your life."

There was nothing I could do to stop them.

Tears flooded free, hot streaks that undoubtedly left rivers of black down my face.

Marks of shame and heartbreak and anger.

My laughter was grim and hurt when I looked at her, the check like a white flag of surrender waved between us. But I wasn't going down without this bitch knowing exactly where I stood.

I tore it into a hundred tiny pieces and tossed them into the air.

For the first time, it was shock that widened her eyes.

"Maybe Paxton chose to use me. But when I told you I didn't want anything from him other than to *be* with him, I meant it. Maybe I saw something in him I shouldn't have seen. Maybe I am naïve and simple and gullible."

Maybe my one wild night had truly turned into a nightmare. Maybe it would cause me the greatest pain that I'd ever experienced after all.

I swallowed around the grief that threatened to spill out. I looked to where the pieces of the check were scattered around our feet on the plush carpeted floor.

"But I will never be this person."

I started for the door, before I turned and looked at her from over my shoulder.

"And I am not for sale."

Then I turned and fled.

eighteen
Paxton

Jackson MacPherson would have talked for another hour if I let him. I feigned interest, but honestly didn't give a shit what he had to say. My thoughts were only on Kaylee and getting her back to our suite. Fortunately, Kenneth stepped in and pulled me away when Jackson showed no reasonable attempts at letting up.

It's been an hour since I saw Kaylee, and my heart beats wildly against my chest as I slink down the dark hallway toward the green room. Never has a woman completely consumed my thoughts like Kaylee has. Never have I wanted to disappear from Hollywood and hole up in a cabin in the middle of nowhere with a woman I met mere days ago…until Kaylee.

My eyes scan the greenroom, searching for her in the sea of bodies that stand sipping on drinks and having artificial conversations about absolutely nothing of importance.

Kendall stands against the far wall, a tall champagne glass propped in her hand as she laughs at something the man she's speaking with has said. Her head bouncing with short bouts of laughter until she sees me. She stands up straighter, raising her chin when she sees me approach, my eyes still scanning the room for Kaylee.

"Where's Kay?" I ask, not giving a fuck about interrupting her conversation.

"Don't be rude," she scolds me, cocking an eyebrow and pursing her lips. "Paxton, this is Ransom Jae." I've heard the name before. Some new fucking Hollywood guy that everyone seems to be getting their shit in a twist over. Honestly, he looks like a boy-band dropout, nothing that really sets him apart from every other twenty-something Hollywood actor.

"What's up?" I ask, looking over his shoulder for Kaylee only to see the crowd in the room thinning as everyone begins to head out to one of the many after parties that follow these screenings. Just like the one where I met Kaylee.

Where is she?

I turn around, pinching my bottom lip between my fingers as I try to figure out where she could be. My feet shuffle across the carpet to Kenneth who stands crouched down picking up little pieces of paper off the floor with his right hand, with a cell phone still pressed to his ear with his left.

He freezes as my feet stop just inches from his fingers. "I have to go," I hear him say with his thick British accent, as he shoves his phone down into one of his suit-jacket pockets.

"What are you doing?" I ask him as he stands straight up, his eyes meeting mine. His face is void of any expression as he swallows hard, his Adams apple bouncing nervously in his throat.

It's as if he's looking through me, and I turn around to see what he's looking at.

Or rather, who.

Kendall stands tall, her shoulders square with her head shaking from side to side in a silent warning to Kenneth.

He inhales and narrows his eyes at Kendall, a war of unspoken words raging between the two of them. "I think you'll want this," he says, quietly dropping the pieces of paper into my hand. "I'm going to see if I can find Kaylee." He shoots a pointed look over my shoulder directly at Kendall as I decipher what in the hell is happening.

I look at the palm of my hand with shreds of paper, and I can tell I'm holding a check, but what it's for is beyond me. As I inspect the pieces more closely, I can see the letters 'Kay' handwritten in

Kendall's distinct handwriting.

I turn around to see Kendall standing tall in defiance, her chin raised as I slowly begin to piece everything together.

"Where's Kaylee," I ask again through gritted teeth. Kendall's obstinance is starting to wear on my nerves as anger begins to set in. I'm done fucking around with Kendall and her petty bullshit.

She waves her free hand dismissing my concern. "She's headed back to the States, where she belongs. This charade needed to end, so I ended it." Her lips twist into a fake smile before she finishes off the rest of her champagne, smacking her lips when she finishes.

With one long stride, I reach out and grab Kendall's arm, never having touched a woman in such an aggressive manner before. The delicate champagne glass falls from her hand and to the floor, shattering into a million little pieces at our feet.

"Pax!" she says with a hush as I yank her toward me.

"Where the fuck is she," I bark at her, causing her eyes to widen in fear. I've let Kendall run the show for too fucking long. She's my publicist, not my handler.

"Probably on her way to the airport right about now." She glances at the large clock on the wall in the green room. "Her flight is scheduled to leave in an hour."

An hour. Sixty minutes. There is no way I'll make it to Heathrow in sixty minutes at this time of day. I squeeze Kendall's arm, and she gasps, "You're fired!" I tell her, anger seething with every word.

"You have crossed the line, Kendall. For years, I have been patient with you, allowing you to make decisions that weren't yours to make. I trusted you, as my publicist to have my back. But this…you know how I feel about Kaylee. I told you what I had with Kaylee was different and you were so threatened by that, that you just had to try and destroy the one thing that has made me genuinely happy. Well, fuck you, Kendall. Fuck you."

I spit the words in her face. Her eyes wide at my outburst. I release her arm and take a step backward as I try to figure out how in the hell I can get to Kaylee.

"Kenneth!" I shout and he appears at my side almost instantly.

"I'm already on it," he cuts in. "I'm making calls to every airline.

I don't know that they'll stop her from boarding, but I'll do my best." He offers me a sympathetic look. "I've already requested Ronald bring the car around. He'll meet out the back entrance."

I nod in appreciation. Thank God for Kenneth.

"This way." He points to a door that will take us out the back way.

The alley smells of piss and garbage, but Ronald is waiting with the door open when we exit the back of the theater. He hurries us inside the car while Kenneth continues to call every airline with flights to the United States.

Meanwhile, I'm blowing up Kaylee's phone with texts and phone calls, only each one is met with a return message that I've been blocked.

"Fuck!" I scream and toss my phone across the limo to the seat next to Kenneth. He eyes me carefully as he continues to speak in a professional tone.

"I'm looking for a passenger, Kaylee Burton. She's left something here in London that we're trying to get to her before she leaves," he speaks calmly and professionally. "Yes, I understand you can't tell me if she's on your flight..." I can hear his voice growing more agitated with each call and my anxiety continues to spiral out of control.

"Then tell me what flights you have leaving Heathrow to anywhere in the U.S. tonight?" he asks. His pen anxiously tapping a small leather-bound notebook on his lap. "Fourteen fifty-two to LaGuardia, what time? Nope. What else?"

He chances a quick glance at me as I grow more agitated by every passing second. My hands are balled into fists at my side and I take long breaths as I try to calm myself.

"Flight eight-hundred to Los Angeles at eleven o'clock." His voices hitches, and he looks at the watch on his wrist before scribbling down the information. "Thank you." He sets his phone down on the notebook.

"No one will tell us what flight she's on. I've checked with every airline and American is the only with a flight tonight that leaves in about forty minutes. That has to be the one she's on."

I nod and swallow hard. "Good work, Kenneth," I'm barely

able to muster through my anger-ridden anxiety. Ronald weaves in and out of traffic, but with every stoplight we hit, my hope grows weaker at catching Kaylee before she leaves.

Kenneth taps out messages and makes hushed calls as I stare out the window as rain begins to fall. I count the beads of water that fall against the tinted window, losing count somewhere in the three hundreds.

My anger has turned to sadness, and my hope quickly dissolves as we enter the departures area of Heathrow airport. How Ronald weaves this beast of a car in and out of the traffic is beyond me, but he manages to get me right up to the American departures curb.

I jump from the car and Kenneth is hot on my heels. He hands me my phone and tells me a boarding pass is waiting for me in my email. I jog through the airport, and I begin to see flashing lights and shrills of excitement as I approach a security checkpoint. I tap my phone, pulling up my email, and I see Kenneth pleading with an official looking man.

It's rare that I fly commercial flights and I'm usually ushered from one private lounge to the next as I board private planes owned by production studios and other Hollywood elite. This trip was one of the rare cases.

I feign a happy smile as people try to take my picture and shout my name from their spots in the security line. When security staff assess the commotion I'm causing, they make an exception and take me through a side entrance for a quick and private screening. I owe Kenneth a raise. A big one, if I can make it to Kaylee in time. He nods at me from the other side of security and motions for me to call him with an update.

My hearts races, as the flight door should be closing in approximately two minutes, and I have to make it across the terminal to her gate.

I jump on a motorized cart and offer the driver more money than he probably makes in a month to get me across the airport to her gate. We weave through crowds of travelers, the cart swaying with each sharp turn. My heart beats rapidly as the shrill horn beeps in warning of our approach.

The cart comes to a sudden halt at the furthest gate, and the driver points excitedly at the door that's already been closed. I leap from the cart and nearly knock over casual travelers standing in the gate area.

I slap my hand on the desk and the gate agent quickly looks up from her computer. "How may I help you, sir?" she asks with her thick British accent.

"I need to get on that flight, I have a seat." I shove my phone in her face with the boarding pass loaded. She shakes her head without even looking at my phone. "The plane has already pulled from the gate." She points over her shoulder with her thumb. There I see the large white plane backing away from the gate with the lights flashing on the wings.

"Goddammit!" I scream and slap my hand on the counter in frustration.

"Sir!" she scolds me.

"I'm sorry," I whisper. "I really needed to get on that flight—" My voice breaks. "I really needed to get to someone on that flight." I rake my hands over my face and up through my hair as I concede to the flight gods that it's not going to happen.

She smiles sympathetically at me. "Customer service can rebook your flight for you. We have another flight leaving early tomorrow morning." She shuts down her computer and grabs her belongings from under the desk before sauntering away.

I walk, my head hanging in defeat, to the large windows that overlook the gate and runways. The American Airlines flight carrying Kaylee taxis farther away until it turns down a runway, and I lose sight of it completely.

My heart breaks into a million pieces as that metal tube carries everything I never knew I wanted. Without a doubt in my mind, I have fallen head over heels in love with Kaylee.

"I love you Kaylee, and I will make this right," I whisper to myself, only I'm not sure if it's too late for us or not.

nineteen

Kaylee

"What do you mean, it didn't go through?" I screeched, way too high and loud as my fingers curled into the counter. But I couldn't help it. Not with the way a fresh round of panic that surged through my body.

It was like pouring kerosene on the fiery heartbreak that burned inside of me.

Dread and alarm and the threat of hysteria.

Right there in the middle of Heathrow Airport.

Just awesome.

I'd already missed the flight Paxton had been *so kind* to book me, not that I would have taken it, anyway.

Not while I had a scrap of pride left in me.

Not a chance.

At least the paparazzi didn't give a crap about me anymore now that Pax had tossed me aside like a used-up piece of garbage.

A rumble of annoyance rippled through the long line of people waiting to check in behind me.

They were just going to have to wait. Because I wasn't moving from this spot until I figured out a way to get out of here.

I needed to go home.

Where it was safe, and I could leave all of this insanity behind me. Where I could pick up the pieces and lick my wounds, try to heal from a blow that I should have seen coming from a million miles away.

Only I hadn't.

And it hurt all the worse.

The ticket agent cocked her head in her own annoyance, looking at me as if I were daft. "It means, your credit card was not approved for the transaction. In other words, declined."

"Are you sure? Try it again."

A huff from her nose. "I've already run it five times. I'm sure the sixth will not change the balance on your account."

"Please," I pleaded.

With a shake of her head, she ran it again, the saccharine smile she plastered on her face telling me nothing but *I told you so* as she slipped my card back to me. "I'm sorry, but unless you have another means of payment, there's nothing I can do to help you."

I rubbed my temples, fighting another round of tears.

How could this be happening?

A rush of anger spiraled through my senses.

Oh, there was a clear answer for that.

Bottom-line—Paxton Myles was a jerk.

A horrible, terrible, lying, manipulative jerk who'd taken advantage of me.

And I'd let him.

Like a fool, I'd let him, and now here I was, stranded in a foreign country without a dime to my name.

Just great.

Those tears in my eyes burned hot, and I slumped down as resignation came sliding in.

Overwhelming.

Overbearing.

I choked, nodded in acceptance. "Thank you for your help." Really, the only help she'd aided in was driving the knife a little deeper into my bleeding heart.

Reminding me the cost of being a #PaxtonMylesSlut.

Kendall's words rang through my mind like a tease. *Did I really think I was any different? Did I really think he cared about me? Did I really think I was anything more to him than another conquest, easy entertainment, until something better came his way?*

My heart squeezed.

Squeezed so tightly I felt the physical pain of it.

Because I had.

I'd thought he was so much different than the tabloids made him out to be.

My hands were shaking when I slung the strap of my carry-on bag over my shoulder and grabbed the handle of my suitcase. I dragged it behind me, my footsteps weak as I stumbled away from the counter.

I looked around, and a choked cry scraped from my raw throat when it all finally came crashing down.

I had no place to go.

No money.

And I was going to have to suck it up and call Elle to bail me out.

It was all weighted and compounded by this stupid broken heart.

My *free card* had cost me everything.

Away from the crowds, I sank down onto a row of seats and dropped my face into my hands.

I tried to hide it. To keep it quiet. But another sob tore free. This time loud and ripping. Full of the pain that roared inside of me.

It hurt.

God, it hurt, and I hated that it did. But I'd fallen for a fairytale when I knew they weren't real.

With my face buried in my hands, I sobbed. These big, heaving sobs. Scrubbing my hands over my face, I sniffled and tried to compose myself.

It was time I pulled up my big girl panties and figured out a way to get home.

I lifted my head and my shoulders.

I blinked through the tears.

Great.

Now I was hallucinating.

I'd lost my job and my heart and now I was going to lose my mind.

Because my breath hitched when I saw a man riding down the escalator, wearing the same tux minus the jacket I swore Paxton had worn to the premiere, his head dropped between his shoulders while he anxiously roughed his fingers through his brown hair.

Every part of me stirred in recognition.

Stop it, I silently scolded myself, hoping it wasn't actually uttered aloud like the crazy person I was becoming. Because, let's be real, the last thing I needed was to start talking to myself.

Then the man's head snapped up.

Brown eyes.

Chiseled face.

The man who owned hearts around the world.

Most notably mine.

Shock flashed across his face, before it shifted into the most striking sort of relief.

It was all mixed with remorse and a hundred apologies.

My heart thudded in my chest.

It was him.

It was really him.

And I didn't know if I wanted to drop to my knees in my own relief or rush across the floor and pound my fists into his chest.

Or maybe kiss him and beg him to never let me go.

Because the hurt and shame he'd caused me still tumbled through me like jagged, sharp rocks that scraped my insides, while hope blossomed bright.

He was there.

He stepped off the escalator and then stopped, staring at me from across the space. Unable to stop myself, I pushed to my feet, the breaths jutting from my lungs.

Hurt and hope and this love I shouldn't feel spun around me like a windstorm.

They filled the air between us, and for the longest time, we just stood there...staring.

As if we were both trying to catch up to the moment.

Then his feet were moving, long strides eating up the floor, before his big hands were on my face and his mouth was on mine and he was kissing me.

Kissing me possessively and tenderly at the same time.

I gasped out, my hands curling in the fabric of his shirt.

"Oh, God, Kaylee…I thought I'd lost you. Fuck, I thought I'd lost you. Thank God, thank God." The words were a rumble against my lips, and confusion spun through my mind.

"Why?" The cry escaped up my throat. "Why would you do this to me?"

Why did you change your mind? Why are you here?

He pulled back, still holding my face in his hands. "How could you think I would? After everything I told you, Kaylee? You really think I'd offer you a check as a parting gift?"

"I…" I stammered, searching the sincerity of his face.

"Kendall has always thought she knows what's best for me. She's been controlling my life for years, and I've let her. Because none of that shit really mattered to me, Kaylee. I let her make decisions for me, because in the end, it didn't matter because I didn't care. Nothing mattered. Not until you."

"Oh." It left me on a shocked breath.

He dropped his forehead to mine. "She's gone, Kaylee. The second I found out what she did, I fired her, because I won't let anything come between you and me." He pulled back, those eyes latching on mine. "Do you understand what I'm telling you?"

I blinked up at him, my heart a stampede in my chest. "You want me?" I whispered.

"Fuck. Do I want you?" His brow pinched and he tightened his hold. "I fucking love you, Kaylee. I fucking love you the way I've never loved anyone, and I'm not going to let you go. Tell me you feel the same. Tell me all this bullshit is worth it."

"You're worth everything." The words were soggy, and my hands were shaking when I reached up and scratched my nails across his perfect jaw. "Everything. I love you so much. So much it should be impossible, but that doesn't mean it's not true."

"Oh, thank God." Quickly, he wrapped me up in his arms, my arms pinned between us as if he wanted to grab onto every part of me, the man holding me so tight it almost hurt.

Kind of the way I loved him.

I could feel his smile at the top of my head. "Good…now that that's cleared up, I'm taking you back to the hotel so I can fuck you until you don't forget it."

I pulled back and stared up at his face. "I'm sorry…I…I never should have doubted you."

Gazing down at me, he brushed back a piece of hair matted to my face. "It's okay. I never should have left you alone when I knew Kendall wanted you out of the picture."

I flinched. "I never wanted to make things complicated for you."

He grinned that smile that I'd always known would wreck me. "Don't ever stop making things complicated for me, baby. That's just the way I like it. Let the rest of the world think what they like. As long as I've got you and you've got me, that's all we need."

A soggy smile pulled across my mouth. "Okay."

"Come on." He grabbed my bag and slung it over his shoulder, pulled me to his side, and took the handle of my case, and started us out toward the entrance. Kenneth was suddenly there, grabbing my things, sending me a secret smile.

Kenneth loaded my bags into the car, and Pax crawled into the car, pulling me right onto his lap.

Silence filled the car as Ronald drove us back to the hotel, Paxton's hand cinched down tight on my leg the whole way, my arms around his neck.

He said nothing when we pulled to the curb and Kenneth opened the door, Paxton shifting me around to slide out first before he helped me out.

Paparazzi crowded behind a red rope on the sidewalk, flash after flash striking my eyes when we stepped out.

Pax didn't hesitate.

He pulled me into his arms and he kissed me.

Kissed me for the world to see.

A statement.

A promise.

Then, without a word, he pulled me into the hotel, tension binding in the air as we rode the elevator to our floor.

He let us into the silence, and I turned to look at him as he snapped shut the door and locked it.

He turned back to look at me.

The shadowy darkness bated.

The man so beautiful he made me weak in the knees. He started to work the buttons of his shirt. "Who do you trust, Kaylee?"

Shivers rolled. "You," I stammered.

He shucked free of his shirt. "Good. Don't ever believe what the tabloids print or what someone else tells you. If you have an issue or questions, you come to me. Okay?"

"Okay, I promise."

"Good. Now come here…I didn't get to unwrap you from that red dress I've been fantasizing about all night. The entire premiere, the only thing I could think about was peeling it from this body. What a waste," he teased, his voice dripping with seduction. "Put it back on so we can pick up where we left off. I'd been about half an hour from bringing you back here and ravaging you until the sun came up."

A giggle slipped free, and I glanced at where the red dress still lied in a crumpled pile where I'd left it when I'd flown into the room three hours before, a heartbroken mess. I'd changed quickly and grabbed the few things I had brought with me before I was in a cab taking me to the airport.

Who would have thought I'd end up back here?

Sobering, I told him, "When I came back to this room tonight, I didn't think I'd ever see you again."

I watched the thick bob of his throat as he edged closer. "And when I found out you'd left, I knew I'd do whatever it took to find you. Find you and convince you that you belonged with me."

"I think my heart knew it all along. My first instinct was to refuse what Kendall was telling me."

He set his hand over my heart. "Guess this knows exactly where it belongs."

He let his fingertips flutter down my belly.

I shook.

"And I'm pretty sure this body knows it, too."

Beneath his touch, a moan tremored free. "All of me, Pax." I bit my lip and looked him in the eye. "And you...you belong to me."

It didn't matter if he was famous.

Adored by millions.

He was mine.

I flicked the button on his pants and freed the zipper.

Pax chuckled. "Oh. Seems someone has finally figured out what she wants. It's about damned time."

I peeked up at him as I pushed the pants from his hips. "I've always known I've wanted you. I just always thought it was a fantasy."

His big hands pushed up under my shirt, drawing it over my head. Cool air brushed across my heated skin.

"I am a fantasy, baby. Yours. And you are always going to be mine."

I squealed when he suddenly picked me up and tossed me on the bed. Laughter jolted free, and I pushed up onto my elbows and watched as he twisted out of his underwear, a smirk riding his face as his cock jumped free.

The man so magnificently bare.

I swallowed hard. "You are so beautiful."

He dipped down and blazed a path of kisses across my belly, murmuring the whole time, "Not even close to being as beautiful as you."

He dragged down my leggings and underwear. He kissed the inside of my thigh. "Beautiful...."

He pressed another at my pubic bone. "So fucking beautiful."

Crawling onto the bed, he edged up and pressed a kiss right over my heart. "Inside—"

Then he was hovering over me, his face inches away. The man was so beautiful he stole my breath.

"And out."

He cupped the side of my face. "All of you, Kaylee. I love you."

"I love you," I whispered back.

"Good."

I gasped.

It was a gasp of shock and pleasure.

Because Pax took me.

Took me in the way only he could.

Filling me in a possessive thrust.

My fingers sank into his shoulders. "Pax."

"Feel good, sweet girl?" He uttered the same thing to me as he'd done the first night when I'd gone home with him. Somehow then, it'd felt like a threat.

Tonight?

It felt like another promise.

That he'd spend his life keeping it.

"The best thing I've ever felt," I whispered where my face was pressed to his soft flesh at the crook between his neck and shoulder, feeling the erratic thrum of his pulse against my lips.

His arm hooked around the top of my head. He drew me closer, our mouths a breath apart as he began to move.

Deep, slow, possessive.

Mind-altering strokes that marked me.

Claimed me.

"You are perfection," he murmured back. "So tight and wet and hot. Made for me." His mouth moved to my ear, the words whispering across the shell, sending a wave of chills sliding down my body. "Just like I was made for you."

And our bodies moved in the dim lights that bled from the ceiling.

Shadows that became solid.

Bound.

Tied.

Us.

I stared up at him as he made love to me.

For this first time his touch tender.

I sent him the softest smile.

My own promise.

Because my one wild night had become my forever.

epilogue
Paxton

"You just had to adopt two of them didn't you, Kaylee?"

"They're brothers. I couldn't separate them!" She bounces up and down excitedly in the sand as the two little basset hound puppies wrestle with each other at our feet. Two little puppies that are wild and curious and full of energy, and Kaylee's sweet heart just couldn't say no to leaving one of them behind.

Just what have we gotten ourselves into?

"Someone abandoned them, Pax. Who does that? These were the last two at the shelter, and I fell in love with both of them." Her voice trails off.

"You know what I love most about you?" I pull gently on one of the leashes, guiding the little guy I've got on my leash off his brother.

"What?" She pulls the other one away, finally getting them apart.

"Your heart." I've never met someone who is so genuinely caring about everyone and everything around her. Doesn't matter if it's a person, an animal, or the environment. She's convinced trees have feelings. She smiles up at me. "I mean it, Kay." She blushes at my admission.

"You know what I love most about you?" She squints one eye

as the afternoon sun bounces off the Pacific Ocean and right into her eye.

"What?"

"How determined you are. How you never give up. How you fight for everything you want."

"Like you?" I chuckle, and she swats my arm.

"Seriously, Pax. You just landed your dream job—"

"Stop right there, Kaylee. I'm blessed to have this job. I am. But at the end of the day, it's just a job. I can get any other job, any other day. You're what's important to me."

"You're what's important to me, too." She leans in, wrapping her arms around me, tangling the leashes in the process.

"I love you, Kay."

"I love you more, Pax. More than you could ever imagine." I hear her voice crack with emotion. She rests her head against my chest, and I take in the scent of her coconut shampoo. To think I almost lost her because of a jealous publicist makes my heart sink and my stomach churn. But she's here, with me, and I'm never letting her go.

"Kaylee?"

She pulls away, releasing her grasp on me. She looks up at me with the biggest blue eyes I've ever seen. Eyes that I can see my future in. Happiness. Peace. Marriage. Babies. Growing old together. She's it for me. I clear my throat and choke down the growing lump in my throat.

"Marry me. Show me you'll be mine forever."

"What?" she says, pulling completely out of my arms.

"You heard me. Marry me, Kaylee Rose Burton. Make me the happiest man in the world. Be my wife. Be the mother of my children. Be mine. Forever. Please say you'll marry me."

Her eyes begin to mist over, and her hands begin to shake. I pull the small velvet box from the front pocket of my shorts and drop to one knee on the soft sand.

"Kaylee, do me the honor of being my wife. Let me love you forever, and always." I flip the lid open, and she falls to her knees directly in front of me as she reaches for the box with her trembling hand.

ONE WILD NIGHT

A perfect four-carat princess cut diamond sits perched on a simple platinum band. I went for classic and understated, yet stunning. Just like Kaylee.

"Yes, oh my God, yes!" she says, her voice breaking. I pull the ring from the box and slide it onto her left ring finger as tears fall from her eyes and slide down her soft cheeks. I hate seeing her cry, but I know these are happy tears. "I can't believe this is happening," she says under her breath as she wipes her cheeks with the back of her hand.

"From the moment I met you, Kaylee, I knew you were different. You were more than one night to me—you were my future. I knew that I wanted you to be mine forever."

"Forever," she whispers.

"Forever," I respond.

We sit quietly on the beach, Kaylee wrapped in my arms as the puppies rest next to us in the sand. This is what happiness feels like. The woman you love wrapped in your arms, the cast of the setting sun, and sleeping puppies.

"What should we name them?" I ask as Kaylee drags her left hand down the long soft ear of the little guy lying next to her, rolling her new engagement ring between her fingers.

"Clooney and Pitt?" she says with a laugh.

"You want me to show up on set next month and tell George that my fiancée named our dogs after him and Brad?"

She tips her head back and laughs. A deep, resounding laugh. The kind of laugh that tells me she's happy—and I'm so fucking in love with her and that laugh.

"Yes." She twists in my arms and presses her lips to mine. Soft and supple, warm and inviting. "They're cute, just like Brad and George." I shake my head and chuckle.

"Let's go." I nudge her. "We have to get ready for tonight then I have plans for us."

I stand up and brush the sand from the back of my shorts. I help Kaylee up, and she does the same.

"Oh, yeah, like what?" She smirks, knowing damn well what I have planned. Devouring her sexy fucking body over and over again until we both pass out.

"If I told you we'll never make it to the Oscars. Now let's get Clooney and Pitt home." I wink at her, and she smiles back. She knows what she's in for.

I shake my head at the names Kaylee has picked out. Fucking Clooney and Pitt. Only Kaylee could convince me to let her name our dogs after two of Hollywood's leading men.

As we walk down the beach and toward the path to the Malibu beach home we just purchased, I take one last look at the beach, the setting sun, and at Kaylee. Everything in this moment is beautiful and perfect, and I can't wipe the smile off my face.

I step out of the limo and gently help Kaylee to her feet. Before I even turn around, a young voice is at my side calling my name.

"Mr. Myles, I'm Abigail, your publicist. I'll be getting you through the press line this evening." She smiles at me, before looking at Kaylee who is adjusting her dress. "Ms. Burton." She nods at Kaylee, who offers her a hand to shake which she takes.

This is my first big event without Kendall. She was always by my side for premieres, press tours, and award ceremonies, guiding me through the press line and ensuring I was talking to the most influential reporters in Hollywood. I accepted Kendall's resignation after the incident in London, and my agent has been less than enthused that I've yet to hire a new publicist, so he hired one to help me get through this premiere.

"Shall we?" I gesture to the red carpet laid out before us. Abigail raises her hand to stop me, before glancing quickly at her clipboard and back to Kaylee and I. Squaring her shoulders and lifting her chin in a show of confidence, she licks her lips before speaking.

"You two made quite an appearance on the beach today. Puppies *and* an engagement…" She looks up from her clip board through her long lashes at me. "You're on the front page of every entertainment site and not because you're expected to win actor in a leading role." She rubs her eyebrow, looking distressed. "I've given instructions that there are no personal questions, but with today's events, I can't guarantee—"

"What are my odds?" I ask, flashing Abigail a smile. Abigail blinks rapidly, not sure how to answer my question. "What are the odds of me winning? You know, they bet on this shit in Vegas."

She shakes her head and looks at her clipboard as if it'll magically have the answer before she starts pounding away on her phone.

"Relax," I interrupt. The word is meant for both Abigail and Kaylee. Abigail let's out a breath and looks to Kaylee before they both look at me. "We're not hiding the engagement, but tonight is about the Oscars. That's our focus and those are the questions I'll answer," I tell Abigail before turning to Kaylee. "And you. Breathe. Smile. You're beautiful. You're my fiancée, we have nothing to hide. Don't hide your hand or that ring, and you do not have to answer any questions you don't want to. This is just another night, nothing is any different from any other red-carpet event."

Kaylee nods and takes a deep breath and Abigail glances sideways while mumbling, "Just the Oscars."

I can see how this must be overwhelming to both women so I try to lighten the tone of my voice. "Now let's do this, okay?" I tell both of them.

"One hundred to one," Abigail says before leading us away from the limo and down the red carpet past the first group of reporters.

Fucking one hundred to one. Those are my odds. I swallow hard and plaster on my best smile. One hundred and one would have pissed me off last year, but this year…I've already won. I have the most beautiful woman in the world, and that is all I need.

"Paxton! Is it true you and Kaylee are engaged?"

"Paxton! Kaylee! Over here!"

There are literally a million flashes, so many that it's blinding. Kaylee's laced fingers through mine squeeze my hand so tightly it feels like a vice.

We stop on the red carpet and all the reporters huddle together taking our picture. One after another they shout questions at Kaylee and me.

"Are you engaged?"

"Is it true Kaylee is expecting?"

"Will there be a Hollywood wedding?"

"Are the puppies rescued or from a breeder?"

"Are you excited to work with George Clooney and Brad Pitt?"

"What are your thoughts on the scandals rocking Hollywood?"

Question after question is fired at us, and I don't give a shit about any of them because the only thing that matters to me right now is smiling up at me. I'm a fucking lucky bastard for living the life I do. Fame, fortune, and a job most would kill for. But honestly, I'm the fucking luckiest guy in the world because who knew that one wild night could turn into forever.

the end

Thank you for reading **ONE WILD NIGHT**! Did you love getting to know Paxton and Kaylee? Please consider leaving a review!

More From A.L. Jackson

More From Rebecca Shea

<u>Bound and Broken Series</u>
Broken by Lies
Bound by Lies
Betrayed by Lies

<u>Unbreakable Series</u>
Unbreakable
Undone
Unforgiven

<u>Stand-Alone Novels</u>
Fault Lines
Dare Me

About A.L. Jackson

A.L. Jackson is the New York Times & USA Today Bestselling author of contemporary romance. She writes emotional, sexy, heart-filled stories about boys who usually like to be a little bit bad.

Her bestselling series include THE REGRET SERIES, CLOSER TO YOU, BLEEDING STARS, as well as the newest FIGHT FOR ME novels.

If she's not writing, you can find her hanging out by the pool with her family, sipping cocktails with her friends, or of course with her nose buried in a book.

Be sure not to miss new releases and sales from A.L. Jackson - Sign up to receive her newsletter http://smarturl.it/NewsFromALJackson or text "aljackson" to 33222 to receive short but sweet updates on all the important news.

Connect with A.L. Jackson online:

Page **http://smarturl.it/ALJacksonPage**
Newsletter **http://smarturl.it/NewsFromALJackson**
Angels **http://smarturl.it/AmysAngelsRock**
Amazon **http://smarturl.it/ALJacksonAmzn**
Book Bub **http://smarturl.it/ALJacksonBookbub**
Text "aljackson" to 33222 to receive short but sweet updates on all the important news.

About Rebecca Shea

Rebecca Shea is the USA Today Bestselling author of the Unbreakable series (Unbreakable, Undone, and Unforgiven), the Bound & Broken series (Broken by Lies and Bound by Lies), and Dare Me . She lives in Phoenix, Arizona with her family. From the time Rebecca could read she has had a passion for books. Rebecca spends her days working full-time and her nights writing, bringing stories to life. Born and raised in Minnesota, Rebecca moved to Arizona in 1999 to escape the bitter winters. When not working or writing, she can be found on the sidelines of her sons football games, or watching her daughter at ballet class. Rebecca is fueled by insane amounts of coffee, margaritas, Laffy Taffy (except the banana ones), and happily ever afters.

Connect with Rebecca Shea online:

Page **http://www.facebook.com/rebeccasheaauthor**

Newsletter
https://app.mailerlite.com/webforms/landing/d6b1h4

Rowdy Readers
https://www.facebook.com/groups/527432567356595/

Twitter **http://www.twitter.com/beccasheaauthor**

Instagram **http://www.instagram.com/rebeccasheaauthor**

Email **rebeccasheaauthor@gmail.com**

Made in the USA
Middletown, DE
13 June 2018